Frances Eliza Millett Notley

Beneath the Wheels

Vol. 2

Frances Eliza Millett Notley

Beneath the Wheels
Vol. 2

ISBN/EAN: 9783337347178

Printed in Europe, USA, Canada, Australia, Japan

Cover: Foto ©Andreas Hilbeck / pixelio.de

More available books at **www.hansebooks.com**

BENEATH THE WHEELS.

A Romance.

BY THE AUTHOR OF "OLIVE VARCOE," "PATIENCE
CAERHYDON," "SIMPLE AS A DOVE," ETC.

> "The rock, the vulture, and the chain,
> All that the proud can feel of pain."
>
> BYRON.

IN THREE VOLUMES.

VOL. II.

LONDON:

TINSLEY BROTHERS, 18, CATHERINE STREET, STRAND.

1870.

LONDON:
SAVILL, EDWARDS AND CO., PRINTERS, CHANDOS STREET,
COVENT GARDEN.

BENEATH THE WHEELS.

CHAPTER I.

GRACE CHAGWYNNE'S cottage was almost as near the sea as St. Eglou's Hut. It stood on the edge of a coppice, which hid it from the high road, and sheltered it from the north and east. The garden, sloping southwards, was a wilderness of flowers. The stocks and carnations, the myrtles and blue hydrangeas, were a wonder for size and beauty, while all around the little casement there clustered a wreath of roses, clematis, and honeysuckle, which seemed to be ever in bloom.

To this cottage Lord Crehylls rode at a furious gallop, and flinging himself from his horse at the gate, he slipped the bridle round the rough post, and hurried up through the garden like a man in a frenzy of impatience. He knocked again and again, but a blank silence met him on every side. The door in the tiny porch was closed, so were the lower windows; but above, one of the upper casements was open, and the gentle rustle of this against the leaves, as it swung to and fro in the summer wind, was the sole sound that broke the stillness. " Michael—Michael Polgrain!" cried Lord Crehylls.

The birds twittered from out the eaves at the sound of his voice, and the bees, with angry hum, flew from out their hives and circled round and round about him with threatening buzz, then subsiding, went back to their work again, and the old stillness fell down softly upon leaf and flower.

"Grace! Grace! Grace!" shouted Lord Crehylls with all his might, his hollowed hand upon his lips to send the sound far and wide.

Upon this, a little yellow cat sleeping in the sun, came lazily and rubbed herself against his leg, the linnet hanging in the cage among the honeysuckle chirped and wondered at him, and a distant dog in some farmyard upon the hill barked lustily.

" Are they all sleeping, or dead?" cried the young man, in fevered impatience; and stooping, he gathered gravel in his hands, and scattered it at all the windows. Down it came again, rustling on the leaves, startling the frightened birds from out their nests, and shaking a rain of scented blossoms softly to the ground. Then came the old silence, filled with shadows, which crept stealthily about him, lengthening in the evening sun.

Chafing at the solitude, and growing mad beneath this quiet, Lord Crehylls paced the narrow bounds of the garden, till wearied at last into patience, he sat down upon the stone seat in the porch to wait till Grace, or her brother returned. Here, with head resting on his hands, he thought and wondered till he lost all coherence in his thought, and came back again and again to the old question: Had he killed Mathew Carbis? Had that random blow, struck in boyish anger, really been the death of that miserable villain? If so, what had grown out of this hasty deed? What a world of evil rested on his head now—what a mountain of injustice and of cruel wrong! How should he live under it? Yesterday, nay, two hours ago, there was not a happier man in all the land than he. Now he was —— Good heavens! what was he? Not a murderer! He never meant to slay the villain Carbis; and yet he was dead; and Walter Sherborne was dead likewise, and through him.

Breaking off suddenly in his thought, Lord Crehylls gazed about him with vacant eyes, seeing the bees going heavily-laden to their hives against the southern wall, seeing the great netted cherry-tree luscious with fruit, seeing the huge crimson stocks and snow-white blossoms of the guelder-rose, seeing them and deeming all a vision, and this anguish at his heart a dream. For years no cloud had marred the fair prosperity of his life;

day by day no change had come to check the cheerful monotony of his good fortune; all had been as fair, as level, as bright as a green field in sunshine; and as happily common, too; no strange sorrow had broken in upon his peace, no painful romantic grief had touched him since the day, that Mrs. Sherborne's lovely face had faded from his view.   From that boyish time to this day his greatest excitement had been a fox-hunt, his greatest trouble some small petty care, laughed at in a week and forgotten; and all his hours had rolled on in smooth monotony, commonplace and quiet as our dearest happiness ever is.   Only this morning when he rose, all was stable about him as the round world, and trouble seemed as far away as death and earthquake.   No man could have felt his peace more sure, his life-long comforts more certain than were his.   The sun was not more securely fixed in his place than he was, and he would have laughed at any talk of change or ruin.   Now there stared him in the face the direst, deepest woe that could befall a man, and he had to choose between infamy and death, or loneliness and exile.

At this thought he started up, and strained his ears on every side to catch a sound of life. Any break upon this dreadful stillness would be a relief; it was a silence so filled with dire imaginings, that he caught at the twitter of a bird or the rustle of a leaf, to carry his mind away from its agony. Once he stood before the linnet's cage, and chirruped to the little creature as a child might, his thoughts the while being with his own child, and his eyes beholding, not this bird, but a rare golden thrush, dead long ago, which he had given to his wife, then Agatha Lanyon.

On the soft summer sea, in the evening stillness, sound travels farther than on land; and Lord Crehylls, turning from his thoughts of wife and child, started as there broke upon his ear the gentle, measured stroke of oars. Then came a short, fevered time of hope, and after this a little boat rounding the headland near, with two men rowing, and a woman sitting in the stern.

"Thank Heaven!" he murmured, audibly; and the weight upon his heart seemed lighter. If only when Michael came it might be lifted off and flung away, how thankful he would be! Thankful!—that was not the word. There was no word in the whole sum and round of human tongues—there was no word to tell the joy of guilt removed—the rebound of the heart set free and innocent again.

A few minutes more, passing like slow fires over him, and here is Michael's grey-white face, with eyes set earnestly and sadly on his face, and not a single ray of hope over all his deathly aspect.

"Michael! Michael! is this true?" cries Lord

Crehylls, springing towards him and seizing him by the arm.

Michael stood firm and silent as a rock, till Grace and her husband, with a respectful word or two, had passed on out of hearing. Then he lifted his dim eyes and said, slowly, " It is true. I am blind for it."

" True !" repeated Lord Crehylls, vaguely ;— " true, and you are blind for it ? Michael, you were with me in the wood, and saw me hit that viper. You are a witness for me that I never meant to kill him. You saw that I thought so little of the blow—the just blow—I struck, that I walked on heedless, and never looked back upon the fallen reptile."

" I saw it," said Michael, in the same dull, slow way. " And I saw Walter Sherborne dying in prison for that blow. I have seen no sunlight since my eyes fell on his dead face. Mine has looked dead since then. I killed him—I know it. I killed him for your sake. When he was tried for his life I stood by, and uttered not a word."

The patient pain in Michael's voice, the long, slow agony of remorse, that had made his face a wonder, spoke to Lord Crehylls in stronger words than language, and as he listened and looked, a fixed, terrible belief in his own guilt fell down upon his soul in a horror of darkness.

" Oh, Michael, you should have spoken !" he

cried, gasping for breath. " You should have told the truth. The man's death was an accident, an inadvertent blow; it is your silence has made it murder."

In sight of Michael's sufferings this speech seemed cruel, and the ghastly whiteness of his face, so true in its ignorant love, shone upon his foster-brother in silent reproach.

" When I came back, and found *her* gone," he said, in a low, abashed tone, " I guessed she had agreed to meet you in some foreign land, and I would not disgrace you before all the world—I would not turn Miss Lanyon's heart against you, and make her father your enemy."

" Found *her* gone !" repeated Lord Crehylls, catching in agony at Michael's outstretched hand, " Do you mean Mrs. Sherborne ? Michael, I swear to you, as I hope for pardon, I know no more of that unhappy lady than you do. Did you think I would wrong her—I, who struck down her husband's vile companion for the foul things he said, of that poor victim, of their mutual cruelty ? You remember his odious slanders— you remember his insolent words before I turned at last, and struck him with my gun ? I had provocation enough for that wild blow—I, a rash, hot-tempered boy. Answer; had I not provocation ?"

" I thought so then," replied Michael; " but, looking back now upon that time, I don't think the woman worth it.   See, what is come of her false ways and wicked wiles!"

The blood came up in Lord Crehylls' face, and he struck his forehead with his clenched hand.

"Say no more of her, Michael," he cried, hoarsely.   "I cannot bear it.   I have been happy with my wife; my life has been peaceful, easy, and tranquil; but I have never been able to tear that woman out of my heart."

Michael looked up at him with dim eyes, but made no answer, and for a moment silence fell down between them.   Then Lord Crehylls beat at the gillyflowers and stocks with his riding-whip, saying, hurriedly, "I am a fool to make such a confession, but you are the only man in the world, Michael, to whom I would say as much.   I believe there are some memories which cling to us to the last.   My love for Madeline Sherborne has coloured my whole life, and ruined it.   She was a woman whom it was fatal to a man to meet.   Michael, are you safe here?" he asked, changing the theme abruptly.   "Do you forget you are an escaped prisoner?"

"I am safe enough," said Michael, with a glance towards the sea.   "My boat is on the sands, and the *Penkivel* will be here at midnight."

"Here!" repeated his friend.   "I thought the preventive men assailed your craft to-night, Michael?"

A smile illumined Michael's pale face for an instant.

"It was a plot of ours," said he, "to get the coast-guard men out of the way. There is a heavy cargo on board the *Penkivel*, which we want to land safely; so we have put them on a false scent. They'll go to our cove to capture her, while she'll be in another, fourteen miles away. They will only find an old smack of ours in that little bay, with nothing contraband on board of her except a string of French onions, which I suppose they'll hardly trouble themselves about."

"And the attack on the coast-guard station, Michael, to rescue you?" said Lord Crehylls.

"It wont take place to-night, I reckon," answered Michael. "That was a stram (story) made up just to force 'em to bring me down to Crehylls. Old Uncle Jack is a cute hand at lies."

Lord Crehylls had listened, and yet scarcely heard; and looking up with a sudden paleness on his face, he said, sadly, "What is to be done, Michael?"

His foster-brother understood his question too well.

"You must leave England," he answered. "What has his daughter said to you?"

Lord Crehylls told him the choice which Madeline had set before him.

"I feared this," said Michael, speaking rapidly,

" I feared it from the first moment I saw her face : she is resolute and hard as iron.   Before to-morrow comes she will repent that she let you escape ; she will go to a magistrate before the clock strikes eight.   You must leave to-night ?"

" And for ever ?" asked Lord Crehylls, as the colour forsook his very lips.   " Must I leave my home for ever because of a rash blow ?"

" It was a terrible blow," said Michael ; " it made a ghastly cut upon his temple ; so they told me."

" Did you see him, Michael ?" asked the other, in a whisper.

" No," answered Michael, abruptly ; " I was blind enough.   That sight would have taken my eyes away."

Lord Crehylls seized his hand, wringing it tightly.

" See here, Michael," he cried, pitifully, " I never killed the man—I could not have done it ; not meaning it, you know."

" He was found there, where we saw him fall," returned Michael, sturdily ; " and the gash was on his temple.   He is dead, and Mr. Sherborne is dead, and you and I—meaning their deaths or no—are guilty of the blood of those two men. There—that, to my thinking, is the truth of the matter.   And you must bear it, as I have borne it.   I kept it from you as long as I could."

The contrast between the two men told, who

had suffered through these long years of silence, and Lord Crehylls, glancing back on his easy, careless life, shuddered as he looked on his foster-brother's dead-white face. His long slow martyrdom, his great love, and all the agony which the conscience-stricken man had borne in such dumb patience, became visible at last to the eyes of Lord Crehylls as he gazed upon him. And now he wondered that his eyes had been so long holden that he could not see; he wondered that his heart had been so hard, that he had not cared to know. Shrinking through all these long years from the mention of the Sherborne name, he had never asked or ascertained the exact period of that terrible Sherborne tragedy. A three years' absence will make local news faint and uncertain, and the peasant mind is apt to be very vague in the matter of dates, and it was only of his peasantry Lord Crehylls had demanded information. He never asked a question of Mr. Lanyon; he never spoke of the past to him. There had been great bitterness between them in the old days, when his boy-heart was sore with its mad love; and of late years, knowing what Mr. Lanyon knew, it was not possible, that he would touch on a subject, which shook him to the very soul.

"You have suffered horribly for my sake, Michael," said Lord Crehylls, in a despairing tone. He could not say again it was a mistake

to be silent—a blind, wrong-headed, loving mistake ; the man's face was such a quiet, deathly
protest against reproaches, that he held his
peace in pity.

"It is I who have been blind, Michael, not
you," he continued. "But of what use is all
this talk ? I am wasting time. I must decide
on something while I have sense to think. My
brain is growing confused. I scarcely know
what I am saying."

"You must escape," replied Michael, resolutely. "Will you stay to let Madeline Sherborne ruin you for revenge ? Will you help her
to slay your father-in-law and your wife ?"

"Mr. Lanyon !" returned Lord Crehylls,
putting his hand upon his forehead ; "there was
something I wished to say of him—what was it ?
All this misery lies on his head ; he is more to
blame than I. He persecuted the Sherbornes
from the first ; he hated them always. It was a
cruel thing to hunt Walter Sherborne to death
to save a rich son-in-law. I don't thank him."
Cutting at the flowers again, he laughed, and
struck his hand heavily on the gate. "Let me
pass, Michael," said he. "Standing still like
this drives me mad."

He went into the coppice between the cottage
and the road, and his foster-brother followed
him, and laid his hand upon his arm.

"See here, my lord," he said, quietly, "I am

the one most in fault; don't blame Mr. Lanyon
more than me. I should have spoken, you say.
I should have witnessed against you. But I
could not trample on my own heart like that.
I held my peace, and I should do it again if the
time came again. You don't thank those who
have saved you, so you say; but as for thanks,
I looked for none. And for twelve years I
never broke bread in your house, or crossed
your threshold, lest if this ever came to be
known, people should say you knew it too, and
paid me blood money. As for Mr. Lanyon, I
never spoke one word to him till the man was
condemned, then I woke up as from a dream.
Knowing him innocent, how could it come into
my poor ignorant mind, that judge and jury
would find him guilty, and sentence him to die?
I looked for his acquittal day by day, and when
Grace told me what the verdict was, I felt my
heart melt away in my body. Then I walked
through the night to Penkivel. Mr. Lanyon
was there, and I told him all;—how Mathew
Carbis had met you and me in the wood of
Crehylls, and attacked us with foul words, which
you bore with patience, till he uttered Mrs.
Sherborne's name in a vile way; then you
struck him down and passed on, never looking
back to see where the reptile had fallen. I told
him how I ran back a step or so, and saw him
lying by the brook side, very white, with a gash

upon his temple; but never thinking the blow
had killed him, I followed you when you called,
not caring to stay and help a coward. Mr.
Lanyon listened to me like a man with his mind
gone. At first he would not believe a word;
then he said Walter Sherborne's life was not
worth yours, and I must be silent still. He
would go to the sheriff, and get the man re-
prieved. I was to fear nothing,—he should be
saved. He would go to Bodmin the next morning—this was Sunday. I had walked to Penkivel the Saturday night. With this promise I
went away, and, borrowing a horse, I rode
straight to the prison, and got there on Sunday
afternoon. I found Mr. Sherborne dying—I
saw him die. When I rode up to the gaol it
was broad sunshine; when I came away, all
things were grey and dim, and I knew I should
never see the sun again while grass grew, and
rain fell. Riding on in my blindness, with tears
upon my face like a woman, I got back to Penkivel at midnight. I did not know it was night
—my eyes were new then to darkness; and I
told Mr. Lanyon that he, and I had killed
Walter Sherborne. He was a hale man when
I brought him that news, but all his blood has
shrivelled up at his heart since then. I needn't
tell the rest; you can guess it all, surely. He
put it to me thus: 'The man is dead,' said he;
' of what use is it to speak now? And Geoffrey

Crehylls is like a son to me. He is but a boy, and he struck this foolish blow like a boy. Shall we ruin his whole life for the sake of this dead man ? Shall I kill my daughter—my only child—to clear the name of a ruined gambler ? Let all this die away in his grave, Michael, and we two will hold our peace. As for his child, I will be a better father to her than this poor, ruined, reckless spendthrift could ever be.' I listened to his words, though I knew this day would come. I've known it all along, when I've seen you careless and happy ; we can't hold back the bolt for ever—it falls at last ! There, I've done ! I've told you all the story now, except the things best put to it yourself in your own mind. The long fear and sorrow of all these years wont shape themselves upon a man's tongue readily. Speech, as it seems to me, wasn't made to tell our woe, but to hide it."

Michael ceased suddenly, his dull eyes bent upon the ground, and one hand clasping a young sapling with a nervous force, that shook it like a reed. In his great love he had never once looked upon his foster-brother as he spoke, lest a look should be a reproach ; and his voice had kept throughout a tone so humble and quiet, that not a single green leaf above his head had quivered at the sound.

Leaning against a tree, Lord Crehylls listened to him with sinking courage and sinking hope.

This story, which, related here, sounded so true
and sorrowful, would, in a court of justice, be
simply regarded as the excuses of an accomplice.
No one would believe now that he had not
murdered Carbis ; no one would credit the fact
that he had quitted England ignorant of his
death ; no one would believe that he had not
connived at the error, which fastened his crime
on Walter Sherborne.   Striving to think of
himself as he would of another man, striving to
judge of the circumstances as he would if they
touched some other's character and not his own,
Lord Crehylls felt himself condemned, and
wondered only whether he, or Michael, or Mr.
Lanyon, would be deemed the most guilty by an
indignant world.   When he looked upon the
avalanche of woe which would fall upon his house,
he felt he dared not remain and face the charge
which Madeline would bring. In pity to his wife
and child, in pity to her father, the worn, sorrowful man, whose last days would be disgraced,
he was bound to accept the alternative which
Walter Sherborne's daughter had given him.   In
accepting exile, he would himself be the chief
sufferer ; and if grief fell to Agatha's share, it
would be a sorrow without shame—a sorrow less
dire, less terrible than the one threatening her
now.   Then, too, he remembered the letters in
Madeline's hand, and he shivered at the thought
of his mad boy-love being made a theme of

ribaldry by a sneering world. What a testimony, also, these foolish, passionate letters were against him! In what strong language he had spoken there his detestation, his contempt, and jealousy of Carbis! Why, his own words would condemn him a thousand times in the eyes of all, who read them! There was no chance of escape if he stayed. But he would not stay; he would take the mercy this terrible girl gave; he would believe her promise of silence, and he would leave England, and bury this story in oblivion for ever!

All this and more, ten times more, ran through his mind as he leaned against the tree silent; and when at last he looked up in Michael's face, and strove to answer him, his tongue refused its office, and he flung his arms around his foster-brother's neck in a speechless agony of grief.

"I say!" cried a sharp voice; "Hollo there! Is this Grace Chagwynne's?"

Gleaming through the green trees appeared a chaise, with post-boy and smoking horses. At sight of this vision, Lord Crehylls plunged hurriedly among the thick brushwood, and left Michael to answer this sudden hail.

"Yes, this is Grace Chagwynne's," he said.

"Then ask her to come here and speak to a lady," cried the post-boy. "I've been an hour driving up and down the lanes to find this place."

Grace was soon at the chaise-door, and then Lord Crehylls, unseen himself, saw Madeline's

pale set face, and heard her injunctions concerning the letter.

"Give it into Mr. Lanyon's own hands yourself," she said, in her clear, resolute tones; "it
is of consequence that no other person should
see it.   Is Lord Crehylls here?"

"I can't exactly say, miss," answered the
cautious Grace.

"Never mind; he will be here," said Madeline.
"Tell him when he comes, that if he chooses to
read that letter, and seal it up again, he may.
Tell him further, that I have just quitted his
house at his wife's command," and her lip
curled as she said this; "and therefore the
message I expect from him must be sent to me
at Liskeard.   I stay there to-night, as it is the
town nearest to Mr. Pydar's residence, to whom
I shall go, if I do not hear from him before
eight.   Have you perfectly understood me?"

"Yes, miss," said Grace, much bewildered,
and curtseying as she moved away.

"One thing more," said Madeline, and her
quiet voice stayed Grace's steps.   "Tell Lord
Crehylls that, for his own sake—not mine, remember—I advise him to take every precaution
that my letter is not seen by Lady Crehylls.
You, on your part, must be careful to give it
only to Mr. Lanyon."

Madeline could not help the tone of contempt,
almost of hatred, which rang in her voice when

she named Lady Crehylls. In the midst of this tragedy and dire woe, her querulous, childish behaviour to herself had seemed inexpressibly selfish and small, and she despised her for it ;—despised her too much to use the terrible power she held in revenge. No, she would strike for justice, but not for vengeance. Lord Crehylls, listening to her clear, sharp tones, recognised the ring of hatred in them, and judged her differently. To him she was an avenger, from whose face he must flee for his life. How hard and cold and resolute she looked, as gazing through the leaves he saw the clear-cut, marble profile flash by him as the carriage rolled away!

"Michael!" he cried. But Michael was gazing out at sea, with both hands shading his dim eyes, and when he turned at last, there was a strange excitement on his face.

"There's the Revenue cutter," he said, in a low voice. "Some one has betrayed us. When I broke from you at Crehylls, four hours ago, it was to row for my life, with Chagwynne and Grace, to yonder headland, where I had a man stationed on the look-out. I bade him go across country the nearest way to the creek where the *Penkivel* lies, and order her to come round to St. Eglon's Point at midnight, to take you and me on board; but now, unless you mean to be a prisoner to-morrow morning, you must go at once."

"Go at once!" echoed Lord Crehylls.

2—2

" Yes; we must get to the *Penkivel*," replied Michael; " she can't come now to us.   Go home and get money—get all you want—and I will bring a boat round to St. Eglon's Creek in an hour's time.   There I'll wait for you, and at nightfall we can creep safely away."

The unhappy man to whom he spoke had not a word to say in answer.   He read Madeline's letter, and refolded and sealed it.   It did but confirm his wavering resolve to fly.   Then he flung himself on his horse, and galloped back to the home, he was to leave that night for ever.

CHAPTER II

THE strange, troubled look upon her husband's face struck Lady Crehylls with dismay, as, from her window, she saw him dismount and enter the house hurriedly. Yet she did not descend to the hall to meet him; she did not even send for him. Through all the rosy years of her life she had been accustomed to so much attention, so much consideration, that she never thought of having to seek affection,— it had always hitherto come to seek her, and lavished love and happiness eagerly on her fair head. Thus, to her jealousy and sorrow there was added now a sense of wrong—a painful conviction that she was neglected, which heightened terribly the barrier which their late estrangement had set up between her and her husband. Had she been a woman less spoiled by fortune, less petted and beloved, the wall of pride in her heart would have given way before its flood of agony and love, and with her arms about her husband's neck she would have confessed her misery, and perchance have saved him and herself from a life-long woe.

In the overflowing of this great tide of bitterness which had set in upon his soul, Lord Crehylls' most terrible thought was, that he could have no friend, no confidant. A word of tenderness from his wife might have changed this belief, and opened the flood-gates of his grief; but it was unspoken, and he went away in silence, taking her very life with him. He entered her room abruptly, his whole manner nervous, his face haggard and distressed; but, as is ever the case in this comedy of a world, he hid the tragedy in his heart by a few commonplace words.

"I am sorry I was not in at dinner time, Agatha."

"Where were you?" she asked.

"I was at Grace Chagwynne's."

As he spoke Lady Crehylls flushed to the brow. She remembered Madeline's directions to the post-boy, and to her jealous heart this confession seemed almost an insult.

"I suppose you saw Madeline Sylvester there?" she returned, in her coldest tone.

"I did, certainly," he answered, gravely.

"Did she tell you I had ordered her to leave my house?" she demanded, proudly. "Whatever pain your conduct may inflict on me, it shall not force me to endure that girl's presence."

Lord Crehylls glanced at his wife with a sinking heart. Her coldness galled him to the quick. If only a shadow, a suspicion of the truth steeled her soul against him thus, what would her feelings be if she knew all? With trembling hand he grasped the table upon which he leant, while he steadied his lips to speak.

"If your suspicions make you hate Madeline," he said, "the thought of the great power she holds over me, and through me over you and your father also, might, I think, have kept you from insulting her."

Lady Crehylls looked at him wildly.

"Merciful Heaven! do you own it!" she said, in a low, husky voice.

"What can I do else?" replied her husband, with his eyes on the ground. "Madeline said she had not told you; but it seems she has. And yet, Agatha, Heaven help me! I am not so guilty as I seem."

"Not so guilty as you seem!" said Lady Crehylls, rising and standing before him, pale and trembling. "I never thought to hear such words as these from my husband's lips. Is our happiness gone—quite gone?"

"It is indeed," said Lord Crehylls, as great drops of agony stood on his forehead. "I leave you to-night, Agatha. Madeline gives me no alternative. She is peremptory—and who shall say when I shall see your face again? You will forgive me the pain I cause you? You will say good-bye?"

He advanced towards her, but with a dreadful cry she repulsed him, and wringing her hands tightly together, she pushed him from her with passionate despair.

"Are you so lost?" she said, with dead white lips. "Are you so guiltily, so fearfully in that girl's power, that you dare confess to me that you leave me at her command? Good Heaven! has it come to this?"

The look of horror, and of agony on her blanched face pierced the unhappy young man to the soul. He had not thought she would be so hard against him.

"Agatha," he said, hoarsely, "can I help it if it has come to this? I never thought, when I first knew this woman—Madeline——" (he strove to speak Mrs. Sherborne's name, but failed)—"I never thought to love her, or, loving her, that such misery would spring from my folly. I had hoped to find you more pitiful. I take a broken and guilty heart with me into exile. I go comfortless, and I cannot leave a word of comfort here. Say what you think best to your father; as for me, I cannot find it in my heart to give him any message of peace. He knew all this, and, knowing it, married you to me, in pursuance of a selfish ambition, little heeding how he wrecked your happiness. I would not have committed the cruelty of making you my wife, Agatha, for worlds, if——"

Thus far his wife had listened to him with parted lips and wild eyes; but as these bitter words struck her ear, she burst forth into hysterical cries and sobs.

"Calm yourself, I entreat you," whispered Lord Crehylls, in a despairing voice; "do not add to my misery, Agatha. I will write to you from abroad, and tell you all I wish to have done. Take care of our boy."

He strained her in his arms, not heeding her faint resistance, and without another word turned towards the door; but ere he reached it, his wife sprang forward, and flinging herself before him, she clasped his knees with despairing passionate arms.

"You are not going to leave me?" she cried. "Geoffrey! speak at once! You are not going! It is too horrible!"

"What can I do, Agatha?" he asked, in a weak, bewildered way. "Madeline insists on it. And on the whole it is the safest plan; to remain at home would be to disgrace you all."

The clinging arms fell down as he mentioned Madeline, and starting up, Lady Crehylls fixed her eyes on him with a gaze, in which grief, anger, and contempt seemed mingled.

"You are weak indeed," she said, turning from him. "Henceforth you will be a wreck."

" Great heavens ! is it a time to reproach me
—a time to tell me bitter truths ?" he cried,
approaching her pleadingly. " Listen, Agatha.
Keep our misery a secret, if you can. I shall
tell the servants I am going for a cruise in the
preventive cutter ; repeat the same story to
them yourself. I will find my way to some
neutral port, and thence write to you. Take
courage ; all is not lost yet."

He bent over her, and kissed her, not
passionately, scarcely even tenderly, for in his
new-found remorse and sense of guilt, he fancied
his wife had taken a sudden horror at his
presence : it was thus he interpreted her manner,
and hence he repressed his love, and held it
silent within him.

Sunk in a stupor of sorrow, fear, amazement,
Lady Crehylls saw him leave her without uttering a word of the agony pent up in her heart ;
but when the door closed, and he had vanished
from her sight, a sharp cry broke from her lips,
and she rushed forward to follow him, bent on
making a further and more desperate effort to
save him. When she reached the door she
found it firmly fastened ; in closing it a bolt had
fallen, and in her terror and anguish, and haste,
she was long in discovering this ; but, drawing it
back at last, she flew down the great staircase to
the hall, and found it empty and quiet. Breathless,she ran from room to room,through the whole

spacious suite, calling "Geoffrey!" in a hurried voice—a voice whose pain and passion rose to agony, as she found each room tenantless and silent. At length, in the library, the last room in the wing, she saw from the great bay window her husband, half a mile away, riding furiously through the long avenue leading to the lodge. Then a deathly coldness seized upon her, and, without a cry, she fell fainting to the floor.

*   *   *   *   *   *

Lord Crehylls left his horse at the lodge, saying : " Take him back to the castle, and tell Grylls I am so angry at his aiding Polgrain to escape, that I am resolved to recapture him. I shall go on board the preventive cutter, standing off the headland ; and perhaps I shall not return home to-night. Let them know this at the house. I was in such haste, I had no time to say where I was going."

At the last stile, just at the entrance to the wood, Lord Crehylls found his little son. The boy was sitting on the grass, crying lustily.

" What is the matter?" said Lord Crehylls, taking the child in his arms. " How is it you are here alone ?"

" Mary is gone down there," said the boy, pointing to a distant meadow, " and the shadows are so big, I get afraid."

It was just eight o'clock, and the deep rosy

clouds of sunset were spread over the northern sky.

"My dear, you ought to be in bed," said Lord Crehylls, gazing round him anxiously. But the truant nurse was nowhere to be seen. Then, hollowing his hand, he called to her loudly, but in vain, for there was no response.

"Curse the girl!" exclaimed the young nobleman, angrily. "How dared she neglect and leave you like this? Who is with her, Aubrey?"

"A tall man," returned the child. And, frightened by his father's angry voice, he clung to him with sobs and cries.

Furious at the woman's selfish carelessness, Lord Crehylls paced to and fro the field, chafing and impatient, till the boy fell asleep on his shoulder, and still there was no sign of Mary and her tall sweetheart. Then, looking at his watch, he saw it was an hour and a half since he had quitted the cottage, and he dared delay no longer.

"I must take the child on to St. Eglon's Hut," he said to himself, "and send him home with Chagwynne."

He walked on hastily through the wood, avoiding the ford, and only striking the river when far below that terrible spot. Following the stream, he soon found himself opposite the platform, or ledge of rock, on which stood St. Eglon's Hut. The house lay in deep shadow, for the sun was gone down, though on the north-western front, looking seawards, a narrow crimson streak, like blood, ran straight across the windows. All else was dark; and the long, trailing plants, hanging desolately down from balcony and casement, were so thickly clustered together that, as they waved to and fro in the wind, they seemed a funeral pall, fitly covering this dwelling of crime and sorrow. Gazing on the place wistfully, Lord Crehylls stood still a moment, while a shudder passed over all his frame. From this drear spot had risen all his woe. From these desolate and empty windows— blood-streaked by the dying sun—there looked down on him a throng of passionate memories, all culminating in that white, evil face, lying, blood-streaked too, upon the green moss by the darkening river. All the love, all the jealousy, all the agony of that time and of this pressed upon his brain, as his eyes fixed themselves in sorrow on St. Eglon's Hut. From amid the tangled leaves he saw again the small white hand, that had often beckoned to him in false kindness, as in his boyish worship—unthinking as a child's—he had lingered on this very spot, longing for a sight of that rare lovely face. And for this he was wrecked; for this he was now an exile—a ruined, reckless man.

Stopping the current of fevered thought that rushed wildly over his brain, he plunged deeply

into the darkening wood, till St. Eglon's Hut
was lost in the dusk of twilight; then turning
he regained the river side where it widened to a
creek, and the tide came up with gentle ripple,
lapping the large flat rocks which lay upon the
beach.   Here, hidden by a sharp projection of
the cliff, he saw the boat, but it held but one
rower, Michael Polgrain.

"What shall I do with the child?" said
Lord Crehylls, hurriedly.

"Step in quickly," answered Michael; "you
have kept me waiting too long.   If any one on
board the cutter recognises me, they'll chase us."

"The boy! what shall I do with the boy?"
reiterated Lord Crehylls.   Then for the first
time Michael saw him, and stared blankly at his
foster-brother.

"When we reach the *Penkivel* we can send him
home by one of the men, if you wish," replied
Michael.

There was no time for expostulation or
for thought.   Lord Crehylls stepped within the
boat, and with lusty arms Michael dipped the
oars in the water, and gently as a bird she
crept out into the dusky sea.

CHAPTER III

SIX o'clock in the bright June morning, and there came rolling into the inn yard a mail coach with four smoking horses, a coachman whose coat seemed all capes, and his throat all neckerchief; a guard in scarlet, whose chief business appeared to be to blow a horn; and a crowd of Insides and Outsides; the latter cheerful, the former sulky and sleepy.

Madeline, already dressed, looked out from her window upon the steaming horses, led away to the stable, and the fresh horses, with their coats shining like satin, which were brought out plunging, and harnessed to the coach. Gazing on this scene, with its attendant crowd, as on a picture, she saw a gay, careless figure, descending airily from the roof, with a small bundle in his hand. As he sprang lightly to the ground, with an ease and grace which had nevertheless something repulsive in it, like the suppleness of the leopard, he lifted his hat, and displayed a handsome face, full of conceit, impudence, and

swagger. "Good morning, gentlemen," said he,
carelessly. "This is the end of my journey.
I wish you a pleasant termination to yours."

No one appeared anxious to respond to this
greeting; but, in no way discomfited by the
coldness of his fellow-travellers, he replaced his
hat with an air of easy insolence, and turned
to enter the hotel. Then his bold, roving eyes
caught sight of Madeline, and he instantly
leered and kissed his hand with an odious
assumption of gallantry, very trying to the
temper of the bystanders.

"Have you any luggage, sir?" asked the
many-caped Jehu. "Change coachman here,
sir, if you please."

"As for luggage," returned the swaggerer,
"I never carry any more than I can hold in my
hand. Here it is. And as for coachmen, you
may change 'em as often as you like, or the mail
may go on without; it's no odds to me, now
I'm landed safely myself."

He would have pushed by to enter the inn,
but the stout coachman stood his ground so
resolutely that at length he drew forth a re-
luctant shilling, and tossed it towards him con-
temptuously. This he did with a glance at
Madeline, who, utterly contemning his imperti-
nence to herself, had not stirred from her
station at the window.

"Who is that young lady?" he said to

the ostler, as he put himself into what he considered a fascinating attitude. " She's a regular
stunner !"

" That's Miss Sylvester, of Penkivel," returned
the ostler, in a subdued voice. " She came over
from Castle Crehylls last night."

" Castle Crehylls !" exclaimed the traveller.
" Ah ! I'm come down from London on purpose
to see Lord Crehylls. How far is the castle from
this ?"

The ostler's answer was lost in the rumble of
wheels and the clatter of the mail's departure;
but Madeline, who had heard the previous questions and replies, felt somewhat surprised at the
appearance of this strange visitor to Crehylls.
Absorbed, however, as she was in her own
thoughts, the subject did not remain long in her
mind, and soon she forgot it altogether, as, leaning her brow on her hand, she looked sorrowfully
forward to the dim, uncertain future.

How lonely and friendless she was, she began
now to realize. This was the first time since her
childhood that the sun had risen upon her, and
found her homeless, defenceless, and alone. If
Mr. Lanyon had been her father's most cruel
enemy, he had certainly been a friend to her;
his rank, his wealth, his position, had guarded
her with a triple shield, beneath which she had
found shelter, if not peace. Now all was changed.
She was out in the wilderness, friendless, and

must fight her way alone, against the world's hardness and cruelty. Yet she knew, if she published her story, she would meet with sympathy and kindness, and a tide of execration would set in against those whom she had left, guilty but safe. Once more she felt she had been too generous, and she looked at her watch impatiently, longing for the hour of grace to pass. But even before the clock struck seven, a messenger from Lord Crehylls came to her. It was Martin Chagwynne. He brought her a slip of paper, bearing only these words: "By the time this reaches you I shall have quitted England for ever."

As she read this, Madeline sank into a chair, and burst into passionate tears. Was this light sentence on Lord Crehylls to be the only fruit of her father's letter? Why had she comforted herself with this small justice, and left his name and fame uncleared? How foolishly pitiful she had been! She was ashamed now of her weakness.

"I trust there is nothing wrong, miss," said Chagwynne. "My Lord went away last night with my brother-in-law Michael, and I don't think he has returned yet, but I have not been to the Castle to see. Is there any answer to take back, miss?"

"None," replied Madeline, wearily.

"I hope there's nothing wrong," repeated Chagwynne, anxiously. "I have been away all night on Michael's business, so I don't know the news like, and you seem so whisht, miss."

" So this note was given to you yesterday?" said Madeline.

" My lord wrote it before he rode away last evening, miss."

Madeline's lip curled as she heard this. If any doubt of Lord Crehylls' guilt had crept into her heart, it vanished now.

" Would he quit wife, and child, and home so easily, if what he said, and what Michael Polgrain said, of an inadvertant blow, were true?" she asked herself. " No, it is only guilt which decides so quickly on flight; it is only guilt which makes haste to escape, and fears an avenger in every shadow."

Justified to herself by this reflection, she thought of Lord Crehylls' protestations only with contempt and indignation, and wondered more and more at the pity she had shown him.

" The moment I knew the truth, I should have rooted up old feelings and old associations with a strong hand," she cried to her own heart. " I have betrayed the trust my father gave me; I have been cruel to his memory; I have been weak as water."

In the fever of her mind, feeling it impossible to remain inactive, she resolved to proceed on her journey at once; so, dismissing Chagwynne, she rang her bell, and ordered that a place might be secured for her in the coach expected up from Truro.

"It is full inside and out, miss," said the waiter. "They sent us up word this morning that every place is booked as far as Plymouth."

"Then if I post to that town, I shall be able to procure a seat in the stage for London?" she returned.

"Plenty of coaches there, miss : so if you can't get a place in one, you will in another."

"Then get a post-chaise ready as quickly as you can."

Madeline gave the order with a sigh, for her stock of money was not large, and posting was expensive. She began to feel inexpressibly forlorn. Until now no anxiety respecting money had ever troubled her ; but to-day she stood on the threshold of a new life, and she felt she had many lessons to learn. When her chaise clattered into the yard she saw the swaggerer, who had descended from the down mail, standing by looking on while her luggage was secured on the roof ; and when she appeared at the door ready to depart, he came forward officiously, and wishing her a pleasant journey, presented her his hand to assist her into the chaise. Setting it aside quite calmly, too proud to be ruffled by the offensive leer of admiration in his eyes, Madeline bent her head silently to the crowd standing around, and in another moment she had commenced her solitary and self-reliant journey. But the shabby Don Juan, who had molested her, was apparently resolved she should not escape him so easily, for scarcely was she a mile on the road before the hard, handsome, dissipated face was at the window of her chaise. He rode a bony, hired hack, and regardless of the wheels, he brought the poor beast close beside them, and leaning his hand upon the door, he bent his head, saying, in a coarse voice, " I know you, Miss Sherborne. If you had been civil to me, I might have told you something worth knowing. I am a fellow easily won over by a handsome face; but I don't choose to be treated with contempt, so I'll carry my knowledge elsewhere."

Too brave to be frightened, and yet too defenceless to threaten the ruffian, Madeline's face flushed with indignation.

" I am alone, sir," she said ; " a circumstance, of which apparently a coward knows how to take advantage."

Beckoning with his hand for the post-boy to slacken his speed, he put his head still lower, while his over-red lips broke into a smile.

" What a pity you didn't make me your friend," he returned; " we might have gone to London together. A post-chaise for two, eh ? And if I got any luck at Crehylls, I would have paid the piper."

" You had better leave me," said Madeline,

with quivering lips, " or I will appeal to the first
honest man I meet, to protect me from your
insolence."

" Nonsense, my pretty dear ; we are relations,"
he returned, with a loud laugh.   " I knew who
you were the moment the folks at the inn gave
me your history.   A case of conscience, eh, with
old Lanyon ?   His ward, indeed !   Ha ! ha !
I guess the whole story.   Sylvester, too, is a
mighty pretty name, but no whit better than
Sherborne, is it ?   Upon my word, Tom Singleton
is in luck," he continued, and again his insolent
eyes were fixed on her face.   " I hope you'll
marry him for my sake.   Give my love to him
when you meet, and tell him you have seen his
affectionate father-in-law, Dick Rathline.   Ah,
here's the road to the castle.   I'm afraid we
must part here.   Now, if you had only been the
least bit civil to me—I am such a fool where a
pretty girl is concerned—I might have told you
for nothing, a little secret which I shan't sell· at
Crehylls under a thousand pounds.   Wont you
shake hands ?   No ?   Well, good-bye."

Carelessly lifting his hat, Mr. Rathline rode
away, and Madeline saw the easy, swaggering
figure, with head jauntily on one side, going
down the hill towards Crehylls in a blaze of
summer sunshine.

CHAPTER IV.

"HAVE you heard the news?" said Mrs. Gilbert, pulling up her horses with a jerk by the road-side, as Justice Pydar came slowly along in his pony-chaise.

"No. Is Lord Crehylls returned?" he cried, eagerly.

"He will never return," answered Mrs. Gilbert. "The revenue cutter is gone down with all hands on board."

"Good heavens!" cried the old justice. "This is too horrible. Surely it is not true?"

"It is true enough," replied the lady. "I had it from the man who saw her founder."

"And is it certain that Lord Crehylls was on board of her?" asked the justice, dubiously.

"Well, they say so at the castle," replied Mrs. Gilbert, "and I don't see why they should tell any stories about the matter. It seems he was dreadfully angry at the escape of that obstinate smuggler, Polgrain, and he rowed out to the cutter to explain the matter to the officer—at least, that's the tale they told me."

The old justice shook his head wisely, and then remarked, "It is a queer affair altogether. Have you seen Lady Crehylls?"

"No; indeed that was hardly to be expected," said the lady. "She has not seen a soul since the night the child was lost."

"Poor lady!" resumed the justice. "I can scarcely wonder she has broken down. But I hope we shall find the boy in a day or two. We are scouring the country now in all directions, and it is not likely the gipsies are gone far."

"But I don't believe in gipsies stealing children," said Mrs. Gilbert, incredulously.

"Who else could have taken him?" asked the justice. "Those people will steal children for the sake of their clothes, or for the reward offered for them—for the latter, in this case; they hope to make a good thing of it, doubtless. But if I can lay hold of them, they shan't get a penny."

"Then you really believe the nursemaid's story, that she only left the child for a minute, and that she met gipsies as she rushed homewards?" said Mrs. Gilbert.

"I don't see why we should disbelieve her," returned Mr. Pydar. "She is an honest girl enough, and she has been in a frantic state of grief ever since the child was lost."

"Ah!" said Mrs. Gilbert, grimly, "I suppose

it is scarcely wise in this world to say all one thinks; but really, it seems strange————"

She stopped, and looked curiously in Justice Pydar's face.

" You need not be afraid to trust me," observed the old gentleman. " Whatever you say shall never pass my lips to a living soul. I am very careful, I assure you, how and to whom I repeat things."

" Well, it is lucky we are out without any servants," said the lady, " else I could not venture to speak confidentially. You must know that my maid and Lady Crehylls' maid are sisters; and she was down at my place last night, and she says————no, really, I had better not mention it, Mr. Pydar. It is serious, I assure you."

" As you please," said the disappointed justice; " but you would be surprised, perhaps, at a little fact I could tell you. I am not afraid to trust to your discretion, Mrs. Gilbert, though you appear to doubt mine."

Mrs. Gilbert was not proof against the bait. She dropped the rein over the backs of her ancient and dozing steeds, and leaning far out of the phaeton, she said, in a low voice, " The truth is, there is a mystery—a something dreadful, I believe, behind all this. Lady Crehylls does not give any credit to the story about the smuggler; and although the fact of the cutter being lost is not disputed,

I happen to know she has ordered no mourning. She is perfectly distracted with grief; but she does not believe her husband is drowned."

"What does she think, then?" asked the justice, with wide open eyes.

"Something worse," replied his friend. "Don't you think it a curious coincidence that Miss Sylvester has quitted Crehylls so suddenly?"

She asked this question in such a meaning way that the justice could not possibly misunderstand her.

"Bless my soul!" he said, in amazement. "What reason can Lady Crehylls have for such an idea? Miss Sylvester is engaged to young Pellew, you know; and I give you my word she has gone to London. I saw the post-boy who drove her."

"Gone to London, by herself?" repeated Mrs. Gilbert, with immense emphasis. "That is an outrageous thing for a young girl to do. As for Mr. Pellew, I am certain she did not like him. I am certain she refused him at the castle a month ago. If she accepted him afterwards, it was for a mere blind—that's my opinion. But then, I confess, I never liked the girl, or even thought her handsome."

"And has Lady Crehylls this opinion too?" asked the justice.

"And worse even," said Mrs. Gilbert, bowing

her head in assent; "she believes Miss Sylvester has stolen her child."

"That is a little too strong, I think," said Mr. Pydar, flicking away a fly from his pony's ear.

"Ah! I see you take that girl's part," observed Mrs. Gilbert; "but that is because you know nothing of the state of things at Crehylls lately. I can tell you there have been great quarrels between Lady Crehylls and Miss Sylvester, and they've been hardly on speaking terms this last fortnight. Are you aware that the young lady left the castle at the command of its mistress?"

"No, indeed, I had no idea of that; and I am sorry to hear it," returned the old gentleman, "for I think she is quite in the wrong. I believe Lord Crehylls is gone away on affairs of his own."

"Ah, you own that!" exclaimed Mrs. Gilbert. "You don't credit the story of the revenue cutter any more than I do?"

"I have no doubt that the cutter is lost, and I am very sorry for it," said Mr. Pydar; "but, to confess the truth, I do not believe Lord Crehylls was on board of her. Now I'll tell you my little history, and you can draw your own conclusions from it. Two days ago a swaggering, easy scoundrel called upon me, evidently in a great state of bewilderment at finding

the castle doors closed against him. He hinted
at some secret he knew, which, as far as I could
make out, he fancied Lord Crehylls would pay
him well to keep. If my lord had run away, he
could guess why he was gone, he said, with a
coarse laugh. Then he tried to discover if I
knew his destination, while I on my part endeavoured to find out his business. But I could
get nothing out of him beyond the fact, that he
intended to linger about this neighbourhood
until Mr. Lanyon was well enough to be spoken
with."

"Well, and you suppose from all this——"
said Mrs. Gilbert, impatiently.

"I infer from this," interrupted the justice,
"that Lord Crehylls got into some scrape years
ago, the consequences of which are pursuing him
now. He is just the sort of man to be threatened
and bullied, and made run away, instead of
standing his ground. That fellow who came to
me was a thorough scoundrel, and I longed to
wring his neck, while he swaggered and talked
like a bully. I have no doubt he thinks to get
a little money out of Lanyon for keeping this
secret, whatever it may be; but I shall put him
on his guard, and advise him not to give the
scamp a penny; and I hope young Lord Crehylls
wont allow himself to be hunted and frightened
out of the country by a scoundrel. Had I been
Crehylls, I should have stayed at home, and

kicked this fellow into the river when he came
to me."

" In that case you can't think the matter
very serious ?" observed Mrs. Gilbert.

" Some wild, youthful scrape, most likely,"
continued the justice. " And, as I remarked,
Lord Crehylls is just the man to be frightened
into a rash flight. But, depend on it, all will
come right in a little while. Mr. Lanyon will
pay this fellow, or hush the affair up somehow,
and then you'll find Lord Crehylls will come
back."

" I hope he will," returned Mrs. Gilbert, with
steadfast unbelief. " And you think Miss Sylvester will come back, too, I suppose ?"

" I have no doubt of it," replied the gentleman. " I do not consider her at all answer-
able for the mysterious disappearance of Lord
Crehylls."

" Nor the child's either ?" asked Mrs. Gilbert.

" No," replied Mr. Pydar. " What should
she do with the poor boy ? And we'll find him
in a day or two. The whole county is searching
for him now. The tramps, who have stolen him,
will get lynched when they are caught. Every
one is indignant—every one sympathizes with
Lady Crehylls."

" I should think so," remarked Mrs. Gilbert,
gathering up the reins again. " I wonder she
is in her senses, poor thing. Well, the whole

affair is too mysterious for me. I don't pretend
to understand it—respected, too, as the family
has always been in the county."

"Yes, but they are weak, you know," returned
Mr. Pydar. "There never was a Crehylls yet
with a strong head. You recollect Lord Crehylls
did not prove himself very wise in his boyish
days, when he was frantic about the beautiful
Mrs. Sherborne. By-the-bye, that queer fellow
who called on me raked up that old affair, and
asked me a great many questions about it. I
thought that rather singular. I could not understand how a stranger should know anything
about the murder ; but he was perfectly well
acquainted with every detail."

"Oh, he would hear it anywhere," said Mrs.
Gilbert, carelessly. "You will tell me if anything new turns up?"

"I'll drive round on purpose, if I get any
tidings," replied the justice.

And so this male and female gossip parted.
It will be seen by their conversation, that Lord
Crehylls had been unable to restore his child to
its mother. Scarcely had he reached the *Penkivel,* when her crew perceived she was chased by
the cutter, which, under cover of the gloom,
had secretly followed Michael Polgrain's boat.
The storm, in which the cutter went down the
next morning, was just commencing, and Lord
Crehylls felt it would be unsafe to trust his boy

in a small open boat through such wind and weather. There were plenty of brave hands and hearts ready to do his bidding, but the risk was too frightful. So all sails were set, and the *Penkivel* dashed out to sea, with the cutter in full chase after her.

When the sun rose on that June morning, watchers on the coast saw the cutter, disabled and dismasted, founder in the heavy sea; but many a weary week went by before any tidings of the *Penkivel* reached the hearts, that mourned for her with the sickness of hope deferred.

CHAPTER V

S Madeline neared London, her thoughts dwelt more and more anxiously on Maurice Pellew. She felt instinctively that he would disapprove of her conduct in quitting Mr. Lanyon's guardianship, and in throwing herself thus alone on the world. The explanation he would require she could not give. In her promise to Lord Crehylls she had pledged herself to silence; and in her letter to Mr. Lanyon she had deliberately and explicitly repeated this promise. She meant to keep it. Lord Crehylls, relying on her word, had accepted exile; and Mr. Lanyon, relying on it also, would spend the remnant of his days in tranquillity. To take Maurice into her confidence, would be to yield up all power from her own hands into his; and she knew how he would act: he would put the law in force—the cruel, murderous law, which she hated: he would drag Mr. Lanyon into a court of justice, and make her witness against him. This she was resolved never to do; and by the shudder which crept over her frame at the thought, she was fain

to confess that her heart yearned more lovingly over the bowed, shrinking figure of Mr. Lanyon, than over the wronged man, her father, whom she could but so dimly remember. The first was a reality; the second only a dream, a picture, which touched her imagination even to tears, but left her soul untroubled. The calm affection, rooted in long habit, which she felt for Mr. Lanyon, could neither be shaken by grief nor enhanced by fancy; while her love for the poor wrecked and reckless suicide was the growth of a day, and needed all the strength of her imagination and anger to keep it a living feeling.

When the weary journey was over at last, and the coach stopped at the old Bull and Mouth Inn, Madeline looked around eagerly for Maurice, but he was not there; so no friendly hand nor friendly voice greeted her as she found herself for the first time alone in London. The hope of seeing her lover had cheered her through many and many a dreary mile, and the disappointment now fell upon her spirit like an evil omen; and even when rest and refreshment had calmed her over-tried nerves, the same chill foreboding rested heavy on her heart.

She waited an hour, she waited two hours, and still Maurice did not come; then, with tears held proudly in, she sent for a coach, and drove to that poor, shabby suburb, where resided Mrs. Rathline and her son, Tom Singleton. At the

top of the little dismal row she alighted, and
walked the rest of the way.

The door of the dismantled house stood ajar,
perhaps because the bell-wire was broken and the
knocker gone, and these dilapidations obliged
Madeline to tap with her fingers on the paint-
worn panel. This she did till her patience was
exhausted, for although she heard voices in the
room within, the people there apparently never
heard her, but kept up their eager conversation,
regardless, or deaf to her efforts to gain their
attention. At length, being quite hopeless of
making herself heard, Madeline entered the
narrow passage, and stood for a moment in
silence, contemplating the strange picture, which
to her unaccustomed mind the inmates of the
untidy room presented.

Mrs. Rathline sat in her hard chair, twisting
bits of silk between her feeble fingers ; the children, with a box of sawdust before them, were
stuffing pin-cushions, with much noise and squabbling. On the floor, before the fire, knelt a slight,
well-made figure, toasting a very small chop at
the end of a short fork, evidently much burning
his face and hands in the process.

" Now, mother," he cried, cheerfully, " this
will be done in a moment. Toss away your
work, and prepare to dine like a princess. It
is not every lady has got such a good cook, I can
tell you."

"I know that," returned Mrs. Rathline, in a tearful voice. "There is no one in the world like you, Tom. You are killing yourself for a poor sickly thing, who is weary of being a burden to you."

"Be quiet, mother, do," returned Tom. "I don't look a bit like being killed. I am thinking much more about being married."

"Married!" exclaimed Mrs. Rathlin. "Ah! you mean to Sherborne's daughter, when we find her. Don't talk of that, Tom; you give me the horrors. There is another misery for me. I feel sure you'll marry that dreadful girl just for the sake of giving me comforts."

"Not a bit of it, mother," replied Tom. "Why mayn't I fall in love with her, and marry her for herself?"

"Fall in love with her!—with Walter Sherborne's daughter! My dear Tom, you couldn't possibly!" said his mother, in a tone of disgust.

"Don't make too sure of that, mother," said Tom, in the same cheerful way. "I am afraid I feel inclined to like her already. Poor girl! I can guess too well how sore a heart she must carry in her breast. It is sad enough to have a bad father and a foolish mother, without having to bear the unthinking cruelty of the world, which ——"

"Tom, Tom!" cried Mrs. Rathline, beating

4—2

her hands together, " do you mean that to me?
I know I have been a foolish mother."

"No, you haven't," said Tom, quietly ; "and
there is no one will ever dare say so to me.
How could you think, mother, I meant such
words for you? Now, my dear little woman,
here's your chop done to a turn, and the queen
herself hasn't got a better one."

As Tom Singleton rose from his kneeling pos-
ture, Madeline involuntarily drew back out of
sight.   His words had touched her, and she felt
too agitated to present herself just then.   She
thought, too, that her presence would sadly disturb Mrs. Rathline's enjoyment of the small
dinner, which her son was so anxious she should
eat with an appetite, and Madeline smiled to
herself as she resolved Tom should not be disappointed.   So she went a little way down the
passage, and waited full five minutes before she
again endeavoured to make her presence known.
During this time the talk went on, still about
herself, and Madeline listened to it intently.   She
listened because she wished to understand these
people, and to help them if she could.   They
were the only relations she had in the world,
and different as they were to herself, she yet
hoped there might be some sympathy between
them.   Ragged and poor, and wretched as they
were, they were the only people on earth to whom
she was anything more than a stranger, or worse

still, an enemy ; and so here, in this cramped and grimy passage, she felt less forlorn than she had at Castle Crehylls during the last weeks of her unwelcome sojourn.

"My dear Tom," said Mrs. Rathline, querulously, "you've almost spoiled my appetite by talking of Madeline Sherborne. I know it would be a good thing for us all, but I do so dread your marrying her."

"Don't be alarmed," replied Tom, laughing— "she wont have me. That high and mighty Mr. Pellew scorns the idea of such a thing. Not that I care for his ideas," continued Tom. "I hope she and I will be able to judge for ourselves what we ought to do."

"I wonder Mr. Pellew can talk in that way," observed his mother. "And what business is it of his whether Madeline Sherborne marries you or not? I think if he knows where she is, he ought to tell us. But he was mighty close with me, although he could ask questions enough on his own account."

"Questions?" repeated Tom.

"Yes," replied his mother, "he wanted to know where Mr. Rathline was, and who he was, and where I first met him, and all sorts of things besides. Among others, he was particularly curious about that old knapsack, which I am sure Mr. Rathline has had ever since I knew him ; and then he ——"

"Mother! mother!" cried Alice, "here's a lady knocking at the door. And she has been standing staring at us these five minutes, I do believe," she added, in a whisper.

Shaking the sawdust from her hands, Alice set the door wide open, and Madeline stepped within the room. Then she saw in full light the poverty of the scene—the wild, hard-faced children, in untidy garments; the pale, sickly mother,—the lack of comfort, and all the bareness of their grim misery; but, standing among them, with a glow of light upon his face, she saw too the small, slight figure of Tom Singleton. What a face his was!—not handsome, scarcely even good-looking, and yet so earnest and true and kindly, that every eye lingered on it pleasantly, and even sour lips broke involuntarily into smiles.

Madeline's wonderful beauty, her grace, her stateliness, and perhaps also her rich dress and air of elegance, struck the children dumb with amazement. Mrs. Rathline also gazed at her in weak surprise, and Tom only, coming forward with a deep flush upon his pleasant face, had the presence of mind to offer her a chair. Then Madeline held her hand towards him, and said, softly, "I am your cousin, Madeline Sherborne."

Mrs. Rathline screamed in surprise, while the flush died from out Tom's cheeks, and the hand grasping Madeline's trembled nervously.

"I am glad to see you," he said; "and I wish we had a better place in which to welcome you."

Mrs. Rathline said nothing; her eyes were fixed on Walter Sherborne's daughter in mute wonder, and, to tell the truth, in anger also. She was vexed at Madeline's beauty—vexed that in stature she towered above Tom, and in outward appearance, grace, and elegance seemed his superior.

"Do not apologise," said Madeline. "Your welcome would make any place pleasant."

Tom Singleton's earnest, thoughtful eyes brightened at her words, and his face glowed as with sudden sunshine. But when he would have spoken, his mother broke in upon his speech hastily.

"We don't want compliments, Miss Sherborne," she said, in her sharp, yet feeble voice. "We know this is a room in which a lady can scarcely sit down; and the few comforts we had we have been robbed of by a villain."

"My dear mother," began her son.

"Never mind, Tom," she continued, "I shall tell the truth. Miss Sherborne, we are very poor, but poorest of all in being allied to a bad man. He robs us continually, and the law helps him. A few days ago there was nothing in this room but the chair I sit on, and now that poor Tom has got a few things together again, I daresay Mr. Rathline will come back and sell them."

Rather discomposed by this history of family affairs, Madeline only responded to the concluding words.

"I believe I saw Mr. Rathline in Cornwall," she said.

"In Cornwall!" repeated Mrs. Rathline. "What was he doing there?"

"I cannot tell you," replied Madeline.

As she spoke, Madeline looked earnestly at Mrs. Rathline, but she saw no sign on her feeble and sickly face betraying any knowledge of her husband's motive for visiting Castle Crehylls. To Madeline's own mind it seemed clear as day. This man, by some strange means, either knew or suspected the guilt of Lord Crehylls, and he was gone to wring money from his frightened conscience. She felt glad he would be disappointed—glad the young nobleman had escaped the coarse bullying, and bartering to which the threats of the swaggerer would have exposed him. She knew he would keep silent—his chance of getting money in the future would be lost else—and she had no doubt he would succeed eventually in procuring an interview with Mr. Lanyon, and, by working on his terrors and his feebleness, obtain a liberal sum.

"Let us hope Mr. Rathline will stay in Cornwall," observed Tom Singleton. "I assure you, Miss Sherborne, we are very glad to be rid of him."

"Does he live here, when at home?" asked Madeline.

"No, indeed," answered Tom; "this is my house, and he never ventures even on a visit, except when he is quite sure I am out of the way."

"I am glad of that," returned Madeline, "for I was going to propose to your mother to take me as a lodger; and I certainly could not endure the presence of Mr. Rathline, towards whom I have taken a great repugnance."

"You should never be troubled with him," cried Tom Singleton, whose whole face beamed joyfully as she spoke of lodging with them. Mrs. Rathline, however, looked aghast.

"We have no furniture, no accommodation for you," she said, coldly; "and the cruel will your great-aunt has made leaves us no hope of ever being better off."

"Don't say that," observed Madeline, kindly.

Madeline did not see the effect of these words on her cousin. A hot flush rose to his brow, and the kind, earnest eyes, which to a common observer seemed so insignificant, filled with the light of hope and tenderness.

"But I must say it," persisted Mrs. Rathline, crossly. "You are rich," she said, scanning with a critical eye the purple silk, the plumed hat, and lace mantle which Madeline wore. "You cannot understand our poverty, or tell how bitter is our disappointment."

"You are mistaken," said Madeline, calmly. "I am very poor, and I am at this moment so forlorn and friendless, that if you refuse me a lodging, I know not in this great city whither to turn my steps to find one."

The kind lines about Tom's good-natured mouth quivered, but he did not speak, though he looked eagerly at his mother. She, with feeble hands upraised, gazed suspiciously at Madeline.

"If you are poor, how can you dress like that?" she asked, in a hard tone.

A rush of colour flew to Madeline's face; the rude question shocked her. Accustomed by Mr. Lanyon's bounty, to every luxury and refinement, she had thought nothing herself of her dress; and she had yet to learn that in severing herself from his care, she had quitted the honour and comfort of an assured position, exchanging it for one of doubt, suspicion, and danger.

"I was adopted as a child by a rich gentleman in Cornwall," she replied; "and my education, and all else I possess, I owe to him. But circumstances have arisen now which separate us for ever, and I am out in the world by myself, determined to live by my own exertions."

She could not speak of Mr. Lanyon without some slight quivering in her voice, but Mrs. Rathline's ear was deaf to this.

"Circumstances!" she repeated, as her

pinched, sickly face took a suspicious look. " I can't understand what circumstances could happen to make a man change his mind, after succouring you for so many years."

" Mother ! " exclaimed her son.

" Be quiet, Tom, dear," said Mrs. Rathline, peevishly. " I like to understand things properly. What were the circumstances that parted you, Miss Sherborne ?"

" I have promised not to mention them," replied Madeline, quietly.

" Of course not," interposed Tom, eagerly. " We are strangers. Why should you tell us all your affairs ? Don't you see, mother, how impossible it is for Miss Sherborne to give us her confidence all at once ?"

Mrs. Rathline was silenced for a moment, then she glanced again uneasily at Madeline.

" I don't think you would be happy here," she said. " Your ways are not our ways. You have been brought up by a rich gentleman, you say. You must be used to a lot of comforts which you wont find in this poor place."

" But I am going to learn to do without them," said Madeline. " And being young and quite alone, and you being my only relative, I had hoped you would not be unwilling to give me the comfort of your protection."

She rose as she spoke, as though she thought the conference over and her request refused ; but

Tom Singleton's eager words made her sit down again.

" And my mother will be delighted to be of use to you," he cried. " It is only her fear that you will suffer discomfort here, which makes her appear unwilling to receive you."

" If you have set your heart on Miss Sherborne's coming here, of course I give in, Tom," said Mrs. Rathline; " but she knows well enough there is only one way in which we can all be comfortable together, and to that Mr. Pellew said she would never consent."

Tom's distress was so visible and painful, that his mother checked her peevish voice suddenly, looking half frightened at her injudicious words. Madeline rose abruptly to depart.

" Will you let me know your final decision to-morrow ?" she said, laying her address on the rickety table. " Of course you will understand that I will pay whatever you think fair for my board and lodging."

All this dialogue had been interrupted by the whispering and squabbling of the children, whose remarks on Madeline were quite audible, and of a nature greatly to disconcert poor Tom Singleton.

" She is too proud for me," whispered Alice. " I shan't like her."

Ignoring this and similar observations even less complimentary, Madeline took leave of Mrs.

Rathline, accepting Tom's escort to the coach which awaited her.

"Mr. Singleton," she said, as they walked up the dingy row, "I think it best to speak quite openly to you. Neither you, nor I can help the singular and unjust will which our aunt has made, but surely it need not prevent us from being friends."

"I hope not," said Tom. "I hope, too, you don't suppose that, for the mere sake of the money I thought——"

He stopped, with his kind face in a burning glow of confusion.

"That I could fulfil the conditions of the will?" observed Madeline, calm and cold as an icicle. "No, I have never imagined so absurd a thought resting for a moment in any one's mind."

She did not seem to think she would wound him in saying this, but intent only on what was in her own thoughts, she went on in a quick tone.

"Still, it is very annoying to me, Mr. Singleton, to be made the medium of committing a gross injustice."

"Don't grieve for that," said Tom, softly. "We shall do very well, my mother, and I, and the children. I am used to hard work, and I am promised a rise in my salary next year."

"And, hating injustice," continued Madeline,

scarcely heeding his words, " I have resolved to
do what little I can to remedy it.   By boarding
with your mother, she will have the benefit of
the hundred a year, which of course I mean
to claim——"

" Do you ?" interrupted Tom, wistfully.   " I
was in hopes you would have waited a little,
because you know the trustees can't pay it over
to you until—until——"

" Until what ?" said Madeline, in surprise.

" Until you reject me, or I you ; and you see
we have not proposed to each other yet," returned Tom, in the simplest way, although his
cheeks flamed scarlet.   " Of course I know it is
absurd, and disagreeable, and all that sort of
thing; but still, the trustees must fulfil
the conditions of the will.   You perceive
that."

In the calmness of her pride Madeline heard
this without even a blush.   Tom Singleton
appeared to her so infinitely beneath her, and a
marriage with him was so utterly impossible,
that to converse on such a mere absurdity did not
ruffle her superb tranquillity.

" What you say is very annoying," she observed, quietly; " but if it be true, we had better
get over the preliminaries as quickly as possible,
because otherwise I shall not be able to assist
you at all.   For what I have said is literally
true—I am very poor, and very forlorn."

Tom Singleton glanced at her cold proud face and sighed.

"What do you mean by preliminaries?" he said, very quietly.

Madeline felt vexed at his obtuseness.

"I mean that we must let the trustees know, that we do not intend to fulfil the conditions of the will."

"But I, for my part, can't do that," said Tom.

Madeline's eyes demanded an explanation, but her lips were silent.

"I am sure you understand my feelings," continued Tom, steadily. "I could not propose to you merely for the sake of this fortune. I could only do so loving you; and I have not known you half an hour, so I will not insult you with a pretence of love I don't feel; and if there is no proposal, you see, there can be no rejection."

Madeline heard this speech with intense amazement, but Tom Singleton was too insignificant a person to disturb the composure of her manner. That remained chilly as ice.

"Then I fear my aunt's will can never benefit either you or me," she said, gravely.

"I am sorry to hear you say that," observed Tom.

As this remark appeared to hint at a latent hope, Madeline made no reply, but hurried on a little impatiently.

"May I ask you a question?" said Tom Singleton, timidly.

"Certainly," returned Madeline.

"Is it of great consequence to you to obtain this hundred a year, Miss Sherborne?"

"It is of so much consequence," she replied, a little proudly, "that without it I shall be destitute in this great city."

A moment's silence, and then Tom, finding himself close against the coach, turned round resolutely, and paced down the shabby row again, with Madeline still by his side.

"Miss Sherborne," he said, "that fact greatly adds to the difficulty, and perplexity of my position. Yet I think I know how I ought to act. I am a man, I can earn my living more easily than you can. You are too young and beautiful—it would be folly in me to ignore that truth—to find honourable employment easily in London. Miss Sherborne, if you choose to propose to me I will reject you."

Madeline's surprise conquered her pride this time.

"How can I do that?" she asked, in an amazed voice. "The proposition is ridiculous."

"So you wont propose to me?" said Tom, smiling in spite of himself at Madeline's grave face.

"Don't be absurd, Mr. Singleton," said Madeline, dropping her hand from his arm.

"Surely it is not more ridiculous than my proposing to you, and being refused, neither of us knowing the other," observed Tom, taking her hand again with the most simple frankness, and replacing it on his arm; "it is not my fault, you see, if my old aunt has placed us in an absurd position towards each other. It remains for us honestly to make the best of it; and it seems to me this would be the best—that I reject you, and you take the hundred a year."

"Why should I be so much less generous than you, Mr. Singleton?" cried Madeline, a little passionately.

"Because you are a woman," he said, composedly. "Women are, and must be, always less generous than men. I think you have tried to be just; you offered to lodge with us, that we might share the little income which your rejection of my unspoken proposal was to bring you."

Madeline blushed. This little man, who an hour ago had seemed so infinitely beneath her, had crept somehow up to her level, and beyond it; and now they not only looked at each other face to face, but heart to heart, with this faint light, too, upon her mind, that her heart was smaller than his.

"You make me ashamed," she said, "of a proposition which a short time ago I thought generous."

"And so it is generous," cried Tom, eagerly.

" I would not have you give it up for the world. You will make us all so happy if you come."

"To add to your poverty?" said Madeline, bitterly.

Tom Singleton seemed to struggle for a moment with some painful emotion, and then spoke out bravely.

" Miss Sherborne," he said, " we are certainly poor, and yet not so poor as we appear to be. My dear mother is too sickly and feeble to be a good manager, and so the money put into her hands runs to waste. To make amends for this, and also for the unexpected calls made upon us by Mr. Rathline, I am obliged to let a third of my salary lie untouched. Without this reserve fund, I should have nothing, you perceive, to fall back on."

It called a warm glow of shame into Tom Singleton's face to speak of his own self-denial and prudence ; while it was evidently with a pang of self-reproach, that he confessed to the wasteful weakness of his sick mother.

" If you think that my aid in your mother's household would be worth my board, or could justify your spending the sum you now save, you make, I assure you, a great mistake," observed Madeline. " I am too ignorant to be useful, and I am too proud to live on charity. Therefore, Mr. Singleton, without the hundred a year, which I hope to receive, I shall renounce all thought of taking up my abode with your mother."

"Is that your final decision?" asked Tom, a little wistfully.

"Yes," said Madeline. "Please put me in the coach now."

"Stop one moment," pleaded Tom. "Can't I persuade you to ignore this foolish will altogether, and let my mother and myself be your friends till you can find something to do? Wont you let our poor miserable home be your home till then?"

Madeline's eyes filled with tears, but her purpose was not to be shaken by a few kind words. She thought of Maurice, and fancied his love would be her great aid now, and he would be able to show her some way, by which she could find a safe asylum for awhile.

"No," she said, quietly, "if I accept mere hospitality, Mr. Singleton, I have old friends who will expect me to receive it from them. My view in coming to Mrs. Rathline was to be independent, while at the same time I wished you all to share in the little my aunt has left me."

"And yet to get it you wont propose to me?" said Tom, with a nervous laugh.

"I fear I should do it so awkwardly," replied Madeline, laughing too. "And, besides, I cannot be so mean as to take advantage of your generous proposition to refuse me."

5—2

"Then we must throw my aunt's will to the winds," said Tom, shaking hands with her warmly; "for I am afraid my life is too valuable to offer to shoot myself to make you rich. You will let us see you again ?"

Madeline answered in the affirmative, and scratched her present address on a little card, which she gave him. He was holding it in his hand with his hat still off, and the wind blowing his light hair about his face, when his small light figure and the shabby little row of houses, like a street in a Dutch toy-box, vanished from her view.

CHAPTER VI

THERE was a sore feeling in Madeline's heart as she drove homewards. It annoyed her, that the first offer of succour she had received, should come from Tom Singleton —the poor, insignificant cousin, whom in her thoughts she had always so calmly set aside. The manner, too, in which he had shown her that it was by no means his intention to give her a chance of rejecting him precipitately, half vexed, half amused her. But the smile that moved her lips soon died away in other, and deeper thoughts.

"Maurice!" she cried eagerly, as she entered the little dingy sitting-room. He was standing by the window, and turned instantly to greet her, a shade of pain on his grave, handsome face.

"Are you come to London alone, Madeline?" he said, in surprise, as he put his arm about her and drew her towards him.

"I had no alternative," she replied.

"What! was there no staid servant who could accompany you?" he asked. "The idea of you taking this long journey alone, and in the public stage, too, has vexed me."

"How did you know I came alone?" she asked.

"I inquired for your attendant when I found you were gone out, and then I was told you had arrived unattended," said Maurice. "Where have you been, Madeline?"

"To the Singletons," she replied.

Her hand was still on his shoulder, but her voice had grown constrained. Maurice looked vexed.

"Could you not have waited for me, Madeline?" he said, reproachfully.

"I waited for two hours," she answered, and her hand fell down coldly into her lap.

"I only received your letter half an hour ago," said Maurice; "and its contents have so bewildered me, that I scarcely know whether I am in my senses. You have renounced Mr. Lanyon's guardianship, you say. Madeline, why have you done that?" She was silent. "Have you counted the cost of such a rash deed?" he continued, gravely. "How can a young girl like you face the world unprotected?"

"I must learn to do it," she said.

"My dear Madeline, you would be made miserable in the learning," he resumed, impatiently. "It is not a fitting thing for you to do; in fact, it can't be done. When you have concluded this business of your aunt's will, you must make up this silly quarrel, and go back to Penkivel."

" There has been no quarrel," she replied ; " and I shall never return to Penkivel."

" You are in the wrong, Madeline," he said, angrily. " Quarrel or no quarrel, you must return to Penkivel, until I can give you a home of your own."

" I think we had better discuss all this another time," returned Madeline. " I am so weary now."

" As you will," replied her lover. Then the depressed look on her face touched him, and he held out his hand to her tenderly. " I am afraid I am an unreasonable fellow, Madeline ; but the truth is, I am so vexed that I cannot take you to our house. My mother, father, and sisters are by the sea, and I am at home alone."

" Oh, never mind," said Madeline, carelessly ; " I can stay here."

" You cannot stay at an inn by yourself," said Maurice ; " that is quite impossible. Will you go to your old school ? Mrs. Bryant will be pleased to have you."

" But these are the holidays," she replied, " and she always leaves town then. I only know of one place where I can go. Mr. Singleton and his mother have asked me to go to them."

" To them !" exclaimed Maurice, gazing at

her in intense surprise. "Why, they are perfectly disreputable—a mere set of beggars, or
worse."

"I did not find them so," said Madeline,
coldly.

"I do not speak without reason," returned
Maurice, in a very grave voice. "There can be
no doubt that Mr. Rathline is a bad man, and his
house is an unfitting place for you."

"But it is Mr. Singleton's house," observed
Madeline.

"All the greater reason that you should not
go into it, Madeline, unless you are prepared
to carry out your aunt's will and marry Mr.
Singleton, who must be a very interesting person,
if he is like the rest of his family."

"He is not at all like them," she answered.
"He is very agreeable and sensible."

This praise of Tom Singleton irritated Maurice.
Considering the conditions of her aunt's will, it
seemed to him indelicate.

"If you wish to go to Mr. Singleton's, Madeline, if you are unwilling ultimately to lose this
fortune, of course I can have nothing further to
urge against it."

"Are we quarrelling?" asked Madeline, "or
do you seriously suppose I am going to marry a
man to get money? You know, on the contrary,
how anxious I am to reject at once the conditions
of the will, and secure the hundred a year."

Appeased by this, Maurice returned to his old place by her side.

"We'll manage that in a few days, Madeline," said he.

"I don't think you will," she returned, with the faint flicker of a smile on her lips. "Mr. Singleton says the will gives me no power to reject him unless he proposes to me, and he has not the remotest intention of doing that."

"The impudent scamp!" exclaimed Maurice. "Well, I must look into this. I'll read the will, and take counsel's opinion. But my first duty, Madeline, is to find a safe asylum for you. I must ask my mother to return to town at once, and then you can come to us."

This hospitality, offered late, when Madeline had expected it instantly, struck her ear as coldly given.

"Don't trouble your mother to leave the sea-side on my account," she said, "I can stay here very well."

"No, you cannot," cried Maurice, impatiently; "or, if you do, I cannot visit you without my mother. You are a child in the ways of the world, Madeline."

"I do not understand why I cannot stay where I please, go where I please, and see you when I please," said Madeline. "I take no notice of the conventionalities which seem of such importance to you."

In the fearlessness of her innocence she spoke out her feelings bravely; but to Maurice—a town man—her words seemed bold or childish.

"The world makes them of importance," he said, "and we must take the world as we find it, Madeline. Let me explain, while I think of it, that I did not get your letter, because I was at Hastings with my mother. I only got back to London an hour ago; and the instant I read your letter I came on here. What is this you tell me, Madeline, about the Carbis mystery? What do you mean by saying you have found the man?"

"I mean simply that," replied Madeline, in a quiet tone; but her face grew white as snow as she spoke, as she foresaw how her resolve to be silent would set her in antagonism against her lover.

"And who is the man?" asked Maurice. "I laid hold of the strangest clue to the villain that day I saw the Singletons; and yet it seems you have found him first, Madeline."

"I don't think your clue a true one," she said, in a low, but steady voice; "and I shall feel very grateful if you will not ask the man's name, because I can never, never tell you."

"Never tell me!" exclaimed Maurice. "How can I bring him to trial, how clear your father's fame, if I do not know who the criminal is?"

"I do not want him brought to trial," said

Madeline, in the same low, quiet tone. " The law would kill him ; there has been blood enough shed."

" And for this childish reason you would leave a murderer at large, and allow an innocent man—your own father—to rest under an un-merited stain of guilt !" exclaimed Maurice. " My dear Madeline, it is well the affair cannot rest in your young hands ; let me know who the miscreant is, and I will soon deliver him over to the proper authorities."

Madeline shivered as he spoke.

" I cannot do that," she said. " I never mean to do it. You do not know what dire ruin it would bring down on other heads."

" That can't be helped," returned Maurice, impatiently ; " the law must take its course, and we must do our duty all the same."

" I do my duty in being silent," said Madeline, resolutely. " And I am determined, I will not help the law to do any of the atrocious cruelties it commits, in the name of justice."

This to a barrister—a practical man sufficiently pleased with the laws as he found them—was hard for Maurice to bear. He looked on her romance with a pity greatly akin to contempt.

" Madeline," he cried, " while your peculiar notions remained abstractions, puzzling only your own mind, I could endure them patiently, but you cannot suppose that I, a man, can be set aside from my duty by the high-flown romance of a girl. If you do not tell me who this man is, and relate every circumstance connected with your discovery of him, I shall look on you as mad."

" You have known me nearly all my life," said Madeline, clasping both her hands tenderly on his shoulder, " why should you deem me mad now, because I put in practice the theories which you have known me always to possess."

" I wont argue with you," returned Maurice, lightly shaking her hand away. " We are not in Utopia. The English law demands that an assassin should be given up to justice, and I mean to enforce it. Not for one single instant will I connive at the villain's escape—such a cunning, far-seeing villain too, who has gone scot-free for so many years, while an innocent man has suffered for his crime, and lies now in a shameful grave. Madeline, do you leave me to take your father's part more warmly than his own child? Do I care more for your name than you do ?"

Her heart swelled, her cheeks crimsoned as he spoke, and yet, with a vision of Crehylls rising before her eyes, and the sunken figure of Mr. Lanyon, bent by long remorse, pictured painfully on her brain, she felt the justice she had done was sharp enough. Maurice's words would apply to a common ruffian, but not to a man like Lord Crehylls ; the punishment meted out to him was already dire. A coarse prison, and chains, and the hangman's hands, should not touch him ; these would be revenge, not justice.

"Maurice," she said, sadly, " if clearing my father's name would take the blight from me, if it would wipe out the memory of all my suffering, and make me as careless, as thoughtless, as happy as other girls, I would not even then be tempted to let loose upon this wretched man the fangs of our cruel, blood-thirsty English laws ; but when they can do none of this for me, why should I aid them to slay another victim ?"

" Because it is your duty,—because it is law, —because it is justice!" cried Maurice, impatiently.

" Law, but not justice," said Madeline. " As far as it can be done, I have done justice on the guilty man myself."

" You, Madeline, you !" exclaimed her lover. " What could you do, girl as you are ?"

" Holding the secret of his guilt, I certainly had power to pass sentence on him," she returned—" and I did."

" This is too much," cried the angry barrister. " You had no right! It is presumption—it is madness—the madness of youth, romance, and girlhood."

" I certainly had the right," said Madeline, her face flushing with indignation ; " and I used it—used it far more mercifully than the law would have done ; otherwise he would not have submitted to my sentence."

" So he has submitted, has he ?" said Maurice, sarcastically. " And you, Madeline, with your high-flown ideas of justice, yet acknowledge that you have condemned a man unheard, and found him guilty without a trial."

" Not unheard," she replied. " He confessed his guilt."

" Then the law is more merciful than you. It wont condemn a man only on his own confession. And though you accuse me and it of cruelty, I would not pass sentence on the greatest scoundrel living without a fair trial, and a fair hearing of witnesses on both sides. Now, you acknowledge you have done this."

Madeline's face had grown like death now, and she replied, with white lips, " Not without evidence. I had the testimony of one witness."

" Against him ?" asked Maurice.

" Against him," she answered.

" Now, listen to me, Madeline," continued Maurice, earnestly, " I assert that, villain as this man is, you have treated him less justly than I should. I insist on your yielding him up to a fair trial."

Her white lips formed the word " No ;" they did not speak it.

"Not if you forfeit my esteem by your obstinacy," he said, with great heat.

"No," again, and this time it was spoken proudly.

"Will you tell me what sentence your high justice has passed upon this man, Miss Sylvester? —we wont say Sherborne, till the name is clear."

Maurice spoke with cruel sarcasm, and Madeline felt the blood rush to her heart like a great wave; but her pride was roused now, and she was silent and immovable as an Egyptian marble.

"So you wont tell me," he said, clenching his hand. "Madeline, I will save you from your own folly, in spite of yourself. I will never let go the slight clue I have found, till I lay my hand upon this murderer. Then you shall see that the sentence of the law will be carried into effect, while yours was but an idle breath."

Madeline turned to answer him, but uttered an exclamation of terror, as she saw the face of the swaggerer, Rathline, pressed against the glass. The post-chaise from which he had evidently alighted stood muddy and reeking in the yard.

"There's Mr. Rathline," she said, in a low voice.

"Rathline!" cried Maurice. And opening the window with a strong hand, he sprang out and seized him by the throat.

CHAPTER VII

THE easy Mr. Rathline, taken unawares, staggered beneath Maurice Pellew's hard grip, and uttered a succession of oaths in a choked voice.

"Hang it! is this the way to arrest a gentleman?" he cried. "Let me go, I tell you. I'm not resisting the law. I'm ready enough to go to Cursitor Street in a coach, in a genteel way."

"I'm no bailiff," said Maurice, in great disgust.

"The deuce you are not!" returned Mr. Rathline. "Then what do you mean, sir, by attacking a man in this manner?"

"I mean that I intend to hand you over to a constable on a charge of felony," returned Maurice, sternly.

Mr. Rathline's countenance expressed an astonishment past words, but after a moment's dismayed silence he burst into a coarse laugh.

"Then you have mistaken your man, sir, that's all," he said. "I confess I don't reckon myself among the saints, but I have always kept my neck out of danger."

A crowd of ostlers, post-boys, and waiters had gathered around, and began now to pour so many questions on Maurice that he felt annoyed at his own precipitancy.

"What is the matter?" cried one. "What has he done? What do you mean by seizing a peaceable man like this?" cried another.

"Upon my word, he doesn't know himself!" exclaimed Mr. Rathline, shaking himself free, as Maurice relaxed his hold on his collar. "I'll have you up for an assault, sir."

"Then, perhaps, I shall be able to prove my charge better than you will yours," returned Maurice, calmly. "Do you know anything of a certain hawker, last seen in the wood of Crehylls?"

This question caused a sudden and remarkable change in Mr. Rathline's handsome face. His jaw fell, and his eyes grew fixed, either in terror or astonishment.

"May I ask who you are?" he said to Maurice, in a very low voice. "One doesn't answer queer questions, put in an inn-yard, by unknown individuals."

"I am Maurice Pellew, of the Inner Temple, barrister-at-law," he replied.

"Then, sir, although your manner of accosting a gentleman is not agreeable," returned Mr.

Rathline, assuming his old ease with rather too
much swagger, " I am nevertheless willing to
give you a few moments of my valuable time, if
you will order a private room and a pint of
sherry."

This being done, Maurice rather startled Mr.
Rathline, on the waiter's departure, by locking
the door, and putting the key in his pocket.

" What do you mean by that, sir?" he demanded, angrily.

" I mean," replied Maurice, " that I do not
intend that you shall leave this room, until you
inform me, how you became possessed of a certain hawker's knapsack, bearing the name of
' Nathaniel Strangways, licensed hawker.' "

The swaggerer drank a glass of sherry at one
gulp, and bending across the table, he leaned his
impudent face on his hands, saying, carelessly,
" And what am I to get, Mr. Pellew, by answering your question ?"

" That will depend very much upon your
answer," said Maurice.   " At all events, I can
tell you what you will avoid."

" Pray let me hear what?" returned Mr.
Rathline, with much ease.   " I am a fellow ever
ready to receive information."

" You will most likely avoid a halter, for it
is my fixed intention, unless you reply satis-
factorily to my questions, to hand you over to
the watch on a charge of murder."

Mr. Rathline whistled, then stretched out his hand for the sherry.

"I can't say I've been altogether a pattern in this virtuous age," he observed; "but murder, regarded as a science, has been too high a flight for my lowly genius. May I request to know whose highly respectable and saintly soul, I am supposed to have sent to heaven?"

"I believe the man was a greater scoundrel even than yourself,—if that be possible," returned Maurice, with indignation. "I accuse you of slaying a villain named Mathew Carbis, and of indirectly causing the death of an innocent gentleman, Walter Sherborne."

As Maurice uttered these names, a palpable yet indescribable change passed over Mr. Rathline. It was as though some invisible shadow were lifted from him; his assumed ease grew more real, and his natural swagger asserted itself with an increased impudence.

"You do not appear to be aware," he said, with a smile on his over-red lips, "that Mathew Carbis and I were first cousins—almost brothers, in fact—having been brought up by our mutual grandmother, an estimable old lady, whose death is the only assassination I have on my snowy conscience. I regret to say I locked her up one night in her sedan chair, and left her at the street door till morning, and she died, sir, of that innocent freak of mine."

6—2

"Your jests are exceedingly offensive to me," said Maurice, in disgust. "You can relate your family anecdotes in more genial companionship, Mr. Rathline. I have only to remark, with regard to your relationship to Mathew Carbis, that I believe Cain killed Abel."

"Sir, I am aware that unhappy gentleman had that misfortune," returned the easy Mr. Rathline, "and I assure you he has always had my sympathy. Allow me to observe, however, that Mathew was altogether too cunning a fellow to permit me to knock him on the head."

"Even if you were disguised as a hawker?" asked Maurice, fixing his eyes on him keenly.

Mr. Rathline did not wince in the least.

"It is a disguise I have never tried," he said, carelessly; "it is open to objections. The pack, for instance, might be heavy; then, again, hawkers walk. I never saw a hawker on horseback; and I dislike extremely to walk in a world, where animals with four legs are created, for the express convenience of those with only two."

"All this talk is but shuffling," cried Maurice, losing his temper. "I require a categorical answer. How did you become possessed of that knapsack?"

"Is a hawker's pack such a very singular piece of goods to be possessed of, Mr. Pellew?" asked Mr. Rathline, after emptying a third glass of sherry down his brazen throat.

"Decidedly it is," said Maurice, "when that pack bears the name of a man, whom I suspect to have committed a foul murder."

A slight yellow shade paled the red on Mr. Rathline's face, and again he stretched out his hand towards the decanter; but Maurice drew it out of his reach.

"Pardon me, Mr. Rathline, I await your reply," he said, sternly.

"My reply is, that I deny the possession of such a piece of furniture as a hawker's knapsack, and I don't understand what you are talking of."

So saying, Mr. Rathline threw himself back defiantly on his chair, and smiled triumphantly at Maurice, who rose immediately, and put his hand upon the bell.

"You appear to think that I am not in earnest," he said, calmly; "but you will find I am. If I touch this bell, Mr. Rathline, it will be to send for a constable. A watchman is always close at hand outside this hotel."

At this Mr. Rathline looked somewhat discomfited.

"It would be a very disagreeable thing for a gentleman in difficulties to find himself in quod," he observed; "for although I am as innocent as a sucking dove of all crimes and misdemeanours, I have always a hundred writs flying about my head, and the bums would be down upon me like an unwashed army of vultures. You would not feel disposed, I presume, to become my bail for a thousand or so, if you are the means of getting me arrested?"

"Hardly," replied Maurice.

"Then you perceive, Mr. Pellow, you are dealing unfairly with me," said Mr. Rathline. "You take advantage of my position as a poor and honourable gentleman, in debt for necessaries supplied to a beloved wife and children, in order to wring information from me which I may take to a better market."

"To a better market?" repeated Maurice. "And to whom, sir, pray?"

"Why to Miss Sherborne, for instance," he replied. "Perhaps she, too, wants to find the hawker who crept through the wood of Crehylls on the day Mathew Carbis died. Why should I not go to her? She'll marry Tom Singleton soon, and have money."

"You are mistaken," said Maurice, striving to speak calmly. "Miss Sherborne will certainly not marry Mr. Singleton."

"She certainly will," repeated Mr. Rathline, offensively. "She is just the girl to please Tom—stunningly handsome, and proud as a white elephant,—and if she pleases him he'll have her. Tom is a fellow who always gets his own way."

Maurice could scarcely restrain his anger to the end of this speech.

"You will have the goodness not to mention

Miss Sherborne's name," he said, with his face at a white heat.

"I may say she is handsome, I suppose?" responded the cool Mr. Rathline.

"You do not know Miss Sherborne!" exclaimed Maurice, indignantly.

"I beg your pardon," said Mr. Rathline. "I saw her at Liskeard the other day, and proposed that we should come up to town in the same post-chaise; but not believing I was a relation, she declined."

The easy insolence of Mr. Rathline's manner, as he said this, so exasperated Maurice, that he found no words in which to reply.

"Ah, you are surprised to hear that I was down in Cornwall," continued Mr. Rathline. "And a very disappointing journey it was, too. Lord Crehylls gone away, no one knows where—though some say he has got Miss Sylvester with him, (you know who she is, I suppose?) and others declare he is at the bottom of the sea, gone down in the revenue cutter. Then Mr. Lanyon was so ill, that when at last I did get speech with him, he would not hear a single word I had to say; and no sooner do I mention Walter Sherborne, than he falls down with a paralytic stroke, and I see my game is up in that quarter; so there is nothing left for me but to return to the bosom of my domestic bliss, in the hope of striking a bargain with the lovely Miss Sherborne."

Maurice's patience held out to this, then he seized the swaggerer by the collar, and shook him till he was giddy; after which he thrust him into a chair, and held him down by both hands.

"I understand nothing of the tirade of falsehoods you have been uttering," he said, fiercely. "I require only an answer from you; it is that alone to which I will listen. How did you get that knapsack?"

"It is not mine," gasped the breathless Mr. Rathline.

"No, not now," returned Maurice; "because I have bought it of your miserable wife."

"Did she dare to sell it?" exclaimed Mr. Rathline, rousing his giddy faculties. "How dared she dispose of her husband's property?— a husband's property is not a wife's, it is his own—it is sacred in the eyes of the law. It is robbery if a woman presumes——"

"Cease!" cried Maurice, angrily. "It seems you forget how you sold your wife's goods the other day."

"That's lawful," gurgled Mr. Rathline. "A wife's effects are her husband's. I'll bring an action against you."

A tighter twist on his collar silenced him. Angry as he was, Maurice felt greatly tempted to pommel the miserable coward to a jelly, and it required an immense effort to refrain from striking him.

"Now, listen," said Maurice. " I'll let you speak only to answer my question. If you attempt to say anything else, I shall quiet you thus."

Maurice had a strong hand; and it would have given Tom Singleton infinite pleasure, could he have seen the play it made on the neck of his amiable father-in-law.

"Your wife told me," continued Maurice, "that she married you about fifteen years ago, she being then a widow, in good circumstances; and you were introduced to her by a scoundrel called Mathew Carbis, who was a friend, or pretended friend, of Mr. and Mrs. Sherborne. Are you following me?"

The frightened Mr. Rathline with all his coolness gone, gave forth an inarticulate affirmative.

"No sooner were you married than you illused and robbed your wife," resumed Maurice; "and it was your custom, after wringing a large sum of money from her, to disappear for six months at a time. After one of these disappearances, you returned home with this hawker's pack. You related no history to account for your possession of this article; and, coward and tyrant as you are, no one dared question you; but, demanding of your wife the date of that visit of yours to your unhappy household, I found

it was just one month after the murder of Mathew
Carbis. Now, villain, speak !"

Maurice released his choking grip of Mr.
Rathline's throat, but that amiable gentleman
was so aghast at his wife's delinquency, that for
a moment he still remained breathless.

"I'll teach her to give gratuitous information
about me !" he gasped, indignantly. "I'll let
her know——"

But the grasp was on his collar again, and
with hands outspread feebly he was fain to say,
in dumb-show, that he was ready to speak to the
point.

"To begin with," said he, breathlessly, "I am
not the hawker."

"I don't doubt that," returned Maurice ;
"from the account I have received of the man,
I believe you to be too young for him."

"And I swear to you," resumed Mr. Rathline,
"I never set eyes on Nathaniel Strangways in
all my life. The way I got the pack was just
this : I went down to Bristol to see a friend of
mine, and in an old out-house I saw the knapsack, and asked my friend how it came there.
'Hang it, man,' he answered, 'how it got here
is more than I can say.' Well, all the country
being roused then about the murder of my cousin,
and knowing there was some talk of a hawker
who was missing, my friend and I examined the
pack, and found it marked with the very name

of the missing man, Nathaniel Strangways. This so startled me, that I made inquiries of the servants forthwith, and then heard that they had found the pack three days ago, flung over the wall into the garden. And that is all they or we ever knew."

"Do you mean to affirm," cried Maurice, "that you did not place the affair in a magistrate's hands?"

"No," replied Mr. Rathline, "we were not quite such fools. We fought shy of justices, you see, on our own accounts. And news coming the next day, that Walter Sherborne was dead, I saw no use in putting my own head into a trap just to oblige his ghost."

"So no efforts were made to trace the hawker?" said Maurice, in indignation.

"Not by my friends the justices," returned Mr. Rathline; "but my own efforts have been most exemplary and persevering. I have quite devoted my life to the hunting down of that scamp. I have really sacrificed all my prospects to the cause of justice."

The cool ease and impudence of the man had returned to him, in all their effrontery, and he sat swinging his handsome leg carelessly, admiring the Hessian boot in which it was encased.

"You cannot expect me to believe any of this story without some better proof than your word,"

observed Maurice, eyeing him with grim disgust.
"So I fear I must make you acquainted with a
Bow Street officer, Mr. Rathline."

"Don't hurry yourself," returned Mr. Rathline,
coolly. "Hear my proofs first. The principal
one is, that when I quitted my dear friend's
lodgings I took the knapsack with me—stole it,
in fact—and I have kept it ever since,—that is,
until Mrs. Rathline unlawfully disposes of her
husband's property, and thereby lays herself open
to a charge of felony. Now, why should I keep
that knapsack through all the vicissitudes of fortune, unless I had a purpose?"

"And that purpose?" said Maurice.

"Is two-fold, sir," replied Mr. Rathline.
"Firstly, to find the owner of the pack; se-
condly, to make money by it."

The villain's words were so plausible, so likely
to be true, that Maurice listened with an intenter
faith in him than heretofore.

"You appear to be speaking frankly now,"
resumed Maurice; "but I observe you have not
mentioned the name of your Bristol friend.
Pray who is he, and where is he?"

"Of his whereabouts, sir," said the cool Mr.
Rathline, "I regret to say I am ignorant; but if
he has received his deserts, I would suggest, that
his present address ought to be found somewhere
in the precincts of Botany Bay. As for his

name, that is my secret, and I decline to part with it."

"You mean unless you are paid for it?" observed Maurice.

"Exactly so, Mr. Pellew," replied Mr. Rathline. "I perceive we are beginning to understand each other. Hitherto, you must acknowledge, you have had a disagreeable way of expressing yourself. When an individual feels a gentleman's hands about his throat, he considers that rather strong language; he deems himself ill-used, he wants compensation, and if he possesses information which it would be agreeable to the other to receive, he finds himself with a stronger inclination to withhold than to impart it; unless, indeed, the gentleman, who has injured him, can show that it will be for his advantage to repress that inclination; then, of course, being himself also a gentleman, he is amenable to reason."

"And what are your ideas of reason, Mr. Rathline?" asked Maurice.

"Well, sir, they are rather high at present. I have just had an expensive journey and an annoying disappointment—two items which I must add to the sum total of reasons, which I should require of you."

"I cannot see what your journeys or your disappointments have to do with the matter," said Maurice.

"Pardon me, Mr. Pellew," returned Mr. Rath-line, "they have everything to do with it, since both were incurred and undertaken in this Sherborne business. I had good cause to believe that Mr. Lanyon, or Lord Crehylls, or both, would be interested in ascertaining the innocence of Walter Sherborne; so I cramp my limbs, and injure my digestion and my pocket, by a long journey into the land of wreckers, and there I find Lord Crehylls is gone to the bottom of the sea, and Mr. Lanyon, as I had the honour to inform you, parts with his senses the moment I enter on my business. This last circumstance is a great loss and disappointment to me; and to whom can I look for reimbursement but to you?"

"I can understand that you might have got money from Mr. Lanyon," said Maurice, "so we will count your disappointment there as real; the other is imaginary. Lord Crehylls could certainly have no interest in the murder of your cousin Carbis."

Mr. Rathline smiled, and his lip twitched, as though he enjoyed some jest entirely to himself.

"Perhaps you are mistaken, perhaps you are not," he returned, coolly. "At all events, I charge it as an item, although I shall, of course, in naming the sum, have due regard to the difference between your circumstances and his."

"And suppose," said Maurice, "I refuse you any payment?"

"In that case, I refuse all information," replied Mr. Rathline. "'Nothing for nothing' is the motto that runs round the world."

"And suppose again," continued Maurice, "that I am acquainted with a person, who knows the real culprit?"

Mr. Rathline's careless countenance for one instant took an aspect of astonishment and dismay; then he rallied suddenly.

"You try it on cleverly," he remarked, in an easy way.

"You are mistaken," returned Maurice. "I am not 'trying it on.' I have very lately seen a person, perfectly veracious, perfectly honourable, who has assured me that the true murderer of Mathew Carbis is known."

Something in this speech restored to Mr. Rathline his entire self-possession.

"And, according to your informant, the guilty person is not the hawker?" he observed.

"I acknowledge you are right in that supposition," said Maurice.

"Exactly so," responded Mr. Rathline, triumphantly. "And now I think, if you are in earnest, you will allow me to name my terms. Mr. Pellew, for the sum of five hundred pounds I will divulge to you all I know respecting the missing hawker, Nathaniel Strangways. Further,

I must have the king's pardon for whatever comfort, or connivance I have given to the felon since the commission of his crime. Next, I must be employed to hunt him down myself, being allowed my travelling and other expenses in the chase."

"That last is a singular clause, Mr. Rathline," said Maurice. "May I ask your reason for naming it?"

"Hatred, sir, sheer hatred," he replied; "that is the reason. He has been rich, I have been poor. He has had an assured position, I have been a vagabond. And lastly, he has never let me see the colour of his money."

"You demand a large sum," resumed Maurice, thoughtfully. "I am not prepared to yield to such a demand without mature consideration. I am, on the contrary, more inclined to believe that a short sojourn in Bridewell, would bring you to your senses without any expenditure on my part."

"You make a great mistake," said Mr. Rathline. "Carry out your belief, and you will never hear the truth as long as you live. But I'll give you three days to think the matter over. Meanwhile, I'll stay at this hotel, and consent to your setting a spy over me, who shall watch me night and day."

To this agreeable proposition Maurice ultimately consented, and the bell was rung and an individual sent for who would undertake the charge. He was a cadaverous-looking man of the greengrocer order; but his arms were long and strong, and he had a quick, keen eye.

"I hand over this gentleman to your custody," said Maurice. "You are not to leave him for a single instant in the twenty-four hours."

"Understand," interposed Mr. Rathline, " that I am a gentleman, only I am a little out in the head. I require constantly a cheerful and entertaining companion like yourself, otherwise I am inclined to prussic acid and other strong doses of medicine; so you must look well after me. That accounts in a genteel way for his services being required," concluded Mr. Rathline, in an aside to Maurice.

After settling other items, more particularly the essential one of payment, and also agreeing that Mr. Rathline's inn bill should be set down to him, Maurice returned to the room in which he had left Madeline.

CHAPTER VIII

IT was but time lost, when Maurice Pellew recapitulated to Madeline, the conversation he had held with Mr. Rathline. She understood, or thought she understood, it all, and she did not believe he would divulge the secret to Maurice, while there remained a lingering chance of gaining a larger sum from Lord Crehylls for his silence.

As before, the debate waxed warm between them—Maurice, with his practical views, being of course thoroughly opposed to what he termed Madeline's obstinate romance.

" You fancy yourself generous," he said, somewhat bitterly, " but I truly believe, Madeline, you have acted with cruel injustice."

" You have no right to think so," she answered, " ignorant as you are of all the facts."

" You are too self-reliant, Madeline," retorted Maurice, angrily ; " at your age, to be so resolved, is presumption. How can you think to stand up alone against all the world ?"

Her eyes filled with tears, but turning away, she hid them from her lover.

"I have been alone all my life," she said; "I am not afraid to be alone now, when I know I am right."

"Oh, what mad, obstinate, girlish folly!" cried Maurice, almost beside himself with anger. "See here, Madeline; I love you; I want to save you from yourself. Listen to me, I entreat you. Justice belongs to the State: no individual has a right to wield the sword of justice for himself. You commit a crime in doing this."

But Madeline was as fixed and firm as an Egyptian pyramid, and Maurice beat against her stony silence in vain.

"There is no justice in this land," she said; "all its laws are written in blood. They hang a starving man who steals a loaf for his famished household; they hang a silly girl who takes a sixpence from her mistress's till; they hang a boy who rides away on his master's colt; but they shall never destroy any human life through me. All the way through the length of the land, as I travelled, I saw gibbets and bones swinging in the wind. They sickened my soul, and I tell you, if I had no other reason but that loathsome sight, it would make my resolve, to spare this man the terrors of the law, strong as adamant and iron."

7—2

To argue further seemed indeed useless, and Maurice abruptly changed the subject.

"I am almost sorry, Madeline," he said, "that you have left Crehylls, now they are in such trouble there.   Lady Crehylls must need a friend at present."

"But she would accept no consolation at my hands," returned Madeline.   "Her rudeness to me increased tenfold after you left ; it even went so far as insult, till at length she peremptorily ordered me to quit the castle."

Maurice heard this with a burning indignation, which almost overpowered him.

"Lord Crehylls shall account to me for his wife's insolence," he said, fiercely ; "unless, indeed, he is truly gone down in the cutter; and, in that case, I shall appeal to Mr. Lanyon."

"Who, Mr. Rathline says, is struck with paralysis," observed Madeline, sorrowfully.   "Better let things stay as they are, Maurice."

"Shall I submit to your being insulted before a whole county ?" he asked.   "Madeline, this is more serious than you suppose.   Are you to blame?   Have you offended Lady Crehylls in any way?   I judged her to be a most amiable woman.   I should never have supposed her capable of such conduct."

Madeline's lip curled slightly as she replied, "She is amiable, as all the fortunate and the happy are amiable.   While the sea is smooth, they smile; when it roughens, they seek out the Jonah who they fancy causes the storm, and they fling him to the waves. I am Lady Crehylls's Jonah, so she thrust me from her sinking ship. As for offending her, I am not aware that I ever gave her cause of offence in my life."

"Did you appeal to Mr. Lanyon against her extraordinary behaviour?" asked Maurice.

"No," replied Madeline, "he was too ill. I complained once to Lord Crehylls, but it did but make matters worse."

"How unfortunate Mr. Lanyon is so ill!" exclaimed Maurice. "He would be able to give me the most valuable aid in this Carbis affair if he were well."

Madeline was silent. To speak was only to put herself in opposition with her lover, so she held her peace sorrowfully.

"I will get my mother back to town as quickly as possible," resumed Maurice, "and then you will come to us, Madeline."

Madeline thanked him a little coldly. She could not feel very grateful just then to Mrs. Pellew, for her heart was so full of other things.

"And I hope you will stay with us as long as you can, Madeline, before returning to Pen-kivel," continued Maurice, a little anxiously. He was beginning to feel he had been too heated in argument, too angry with her for those pecu-liarities of thought and character, which had once attracted him, and he told himself he would be more lenient in the future.

"I shall never go back to Penkivel," said Madeline; and her voice faltered. "You must learn to realize the fact, Maurice, that Mr. Lanyon's guardianship no longer protects me, and I stand alone, nearly as forlorn and friendless, as any poor beggar-child selling matches in the London streets."

"You have me, Madeline," returned Maurice, taking her hand. "You must not talk of being friendless; and as for Mr. Lanyon, I am convinced you are very dear to him; and whatever soreness or slight coolness there may be between you now, owing to this strange conduct on his daughter's part, it will, I am sure, all pass away the moment he is sufficiently recovered to act for himself."

Again Madeline was silent; but she felt that her silence was building up a barrier between herself and her lover; and she recognised more nearly the truth of the bitter words she had uttered, when she told Lord Crehylls, that her promise of secresy would separate her for ever from the love of Maurice Pellew.

"Mr. Lanyon is not a man to withdraw his guardianship lightly from one, whom he has succoured from childhood," continued Maurice, more earnestly; "therefore, Madeline, I look upon your return to Penkivel as certain; and you cannot have a happier, a safer, or a more beautiful home, until I can claim you."

It was hard to hear him talk of Penkivel thus, and yet hold in her tears, her indignant sorrow, and all the story of her wrongs; and yet, but for a slight quivering of the lip, she repressed any sign of the tumult in her heart, and answered him calmly.

"If Mr. Rathline's history be true," she said, "it may be long before Mr. Lanyon is better again, if ever; and the distress at Crehylls must be terrible. If he recovers, he will live with his daughter and comfort her. He cannot forsake her for me. There will be no room in his heart, through these sorrows, for a stranger."

It was possible this might be true, but Maurice would not hear it.

"I believe very little of what Mr. Rathline says," he replied. "Depend on it his story is greatly exaggerated." With this he rose to go, but paused to say, "How vexed I am, Madeline, to leave you in this dull room in this dull inn!"

Once more a wistful remorse touched him, tinged with a sort of wonder, that a meeting to which he had looked forward passionately, could have been so marred by discord that love had scarcely found a place, even for a moment, on their lips.

"We will talk of ourselves to-morrow," he continued, with his arm pressed tightly round

her. " We will ' let the world slide,' Madeline,
and remember only that we are together once
again."

For answer she lifted her face to his, pale to
the lips, and kissed him mournfully, like one
saying farewell.

" You are not angry ?" he asked, as his eyes
looked into hers with a sudden deepening and
glow of love.

" No, I am not angry," she replied ; " do
what you may—think what you may of me, I
shall never be angry."

Then her eyes drooped, hiding tears, and his
kiss fell upon her lips again.

" What shall I ever say of you—what shall I
ever think of you, except that you are my
own beautiful Madeline ?—the dearest, the love-
liest, the only woman in the world to me."

These were his last words, lover-like and kind,
yet when he was gone, and the walls of that
dull room pressed around her, Madeline sat with
her brow upon her hand, thinking heavily. She
felt, that between hearing of her friendless and
forlorn fate, and seeing it, there was a great gulf,
and in stepping over this, Maurice had flung
some of his love away.

Was this true ? Is the human mind so in-
fluenced by externals that it experiences a shock,
—a recoil of pain, when it sees its idol no longer
on a pedestal in the temple, but on common

ground, stripped of jewels and of flowers? Hitherto, like a diamond in a fair setting, Madeline had appeared to Maurice, surrounded by every elegance and luxury of wealth—the noble and lofty rooms, which became her stateliness, across which her step moved firmly, the works of art, the pictures, the silken draperies, the glowing colours, the soft lights—all of these, by that curious mystery and deception of the eye, common to us all, had seemed a very part of her, giving her their grace, as she lent them her presence. Now, for the first time bereft of all these, she had seen her lover, as it were, face to face, and she fancied in this dull dingy room her beauty was dimmed in his eyes, and her form had dwindled.

Very solitary and sad, she sat listlessly, with hands lying on her lap, and eyes fixed on the strip of grey sky hanging over the noisy street; and slowly, slowly the visions of the past rose and fell, while the future seemed dark and uncertain as the path of a ship upon an unknown sea.

CHAPTER IX.

"AH! I thought you would be dull," cried a cheery voice.

Through the dim doorway and the dusty twilight there came two figures, growing gradually into the shapes of Tom Singleton, and his sister Alice.

"Yes, I was sure you would feel dull and tired," continued Tom. "Every one does when they first come to London; it is such a great lonely place, you see. So I have brought my sister, and if you would like to take a little walk, I think you will find the air will do you good."

Madeline felt it would be an inexpressible relief to escape from this stifling atmosphere of loneliness and too much thought, but she hesitated to accept Tom Singleton's escort. He perceived this instantly.

"I am not going with you," he said, smilingly. "I will only see you and Alice safely to the park gates, and I will come there again and fetch you in an hour's time."

Almost ashamed now of her ungraciousness,

Madeline gladly accepted this arrangement. In the street there was still plenty of light, and the park was even bright with evening sunshine, and gay with all the rank and fashion of London. It was such a contrast with the dull, dismal room at the inn, where she had sat alone with the heart-ache, that it was scarcely possible to help feeling a little grateful to Tom Singleton.

"Your brother seems very kind-hearted," said Madeline.

"Have you found that out already?" asked Alice, staring at her in an odd way. "You'll say more than that of him, when you know him half as well as I do. Here, you know, we are a queer pair, you and I; if you feel ashamed of me, we can go over there under the trees."

"I am not ashamed of you," returned Madeline.

The outspoken Alice looked at her again in an odder way than ever.

"Ah I see, you are too proud to be ashamed of a little shabby girl. Tom isn't ashamed of me either—he often brings me here; but then he isn't ashamed, out of kindness, not for pride, like you. Look! there's the Prince of Wales! Do you think him handsome?"

"Yes," said Madeline, doubtfully.

"Then I don't," observed Alice, in a downright way. "People say he is the first gentleman in the world; but he doesn't behave half as much like a gentleman as Tom does. I should like to see him working hard to keep a sickly mother, and three dirty little half-brothers and sisters. Bless you! he wouldn't do it."

"Very few would," said Madeline, softly.

"Have you got any brothers and sisters?" asked Alice, abruptly.

"No," replied Madeline.

"Well, unless they were like Tom, I don't know that you lose very much by not having them," remarked the girl, with a tremendous assumption of wisdom. "And I think I can say the same thing with regard to fathers. Fathers now, if they drink and get into mischief, ain't much in a family. I know your father is dead —mine isn't. He comes home sometimes, and troubles me and Tom terribly. If there was a good big tombstone over him, I don't know that I should mind much. But where is your mother? —she isn't dead, is she?"

"I have never heard that she is," replied Madeline, hurrying on faster.

"I am a dreadful girl," continued Alice, peering up into Madeline's face with a grim smile. "I know that there is not a more curious girl than me in London. Directly a parcel comes into the house I cut the twine— snap. I can't wait a second till I know what's in it. And I'm just the same about people. I want to find out all about 'em directly I see 'em.

I'm sure there's some secret about your mother, because I heard my mother whispering to Tom about her. And I mean to get at it some way, so you may just as well tell me right out at once as have it screwed out of you by degrees."

"I have nothing to tell you," replied Madeline ; " for it would be very useless to say, that you are talking rudely, even cruelly. You are too young to understand me."

"No, I ain't," struck in Alice. "And you don't think so, either. You think I'm too common, too ill-bred to understand a lady like you. That's your thought. You might as well have spoke it out, as put it on your face so plain, that a horse might read it."

Madeline could not help a smile at this, and Alice grew instantly more gracious.

"I dare say you are right," she said. "I am almost as vulgar as I can well be. Tom is the only diamond amongst us, I can tell you. He ordered me to be civil to you, and I'm sure I've tried to be. I'd let the wheels of all those carriages go over me, if it would please Tom ; and I wouldn't have asked you about your mother, if I had known it would hurt you."

"Let us make peace, then," said Madeline, offering her hand to this queer specimen of girlhood. Alice took it, staring curiously at the dainty glove which covered it.

"Now I'll tell you a secret," she said. "Tom is waiting at the Park gate this while; it is all nonsense about business, and coming back for us : he is simply standing there, patient as Job. And I hope you'll thank him ; if you don't, I know I shall have just as queer thoughts about your breeding as you had about mine."

Madeline did thank him ; and as they entered the inn, on their return home, she gave him her hand with a grateful look, while Mr. Rathline, furtively watching from the coffee-room window, secretly backed Tom Singleton to win against all odds.

CHAPTER X.

AURICE Pellew lived in chambers, and as he came hurrying down the grimy stairs at about ten o'clock in the morning, he hustled a lank individual bustling upwards in breathless excitement. It was the man in whose charge he had left Mr. Rathline.

"What are you doing here?" cried Maurice, angrily, as he recognised him. "I told you never to leave your charge for an instant."

"He ain't in my charge now," returned the man. "Here's a letter."

Maurice tore it open eagerly, and read this :—

"DEAR SIR,—A relentless fate pursues me. It is ever the virtuous who are the sport of fortune. I was arrested this morning in my bed for the paltry sum of fifteen pounds twelve shillings and tenpence. A mere tavern score, sir; a contemptible debt I had forgotten. When will my enemies give me rest? Oh! that I had the wings of a bird. Please send a couple of guineas by the bearer; and oblige me by coming speedily to the rescue of

"Your very obedient servant,

"RICHARD RATHLINE."

"P.S.—Your bail will be accepted, even if detainers arrive, which, to be candid, I expect; for my enemies are legion, and their spite and malice against an unoffending man are past belief."

Excessively annoyed, Maurice Pellew thrust this note into his pocket, and contented himself by sending one guinea to Mr. Rathline, with a message to say he would call to see him on the following day.

"The longer the fellow is in 'durance vile,' and the more desperate he is, the easier will it be to wring this secret from him," thought Maurice. And in this belief he let that day go by, and also the next, without troubling himself respecting Mr. Rathline.

"He is safe enough," said Maurice, complacently. "He can't escape me now, and a little imprisonment and anxiety will do him good."

So, in the hope of bestowing some wholesome discipline on the swaggerer to the benefit of his impudent nature, Maurice Pellew refused his request, sent by a second messenger in the evening, for the loan of another guinea, and

turned a deaf ear to his entreaties to be bailed
out at once.

The state of the law sixty years ago is a
matter of wonder to us of the present day. Yet
the people seem to have borne with it patiently,
and like Goldsmith's imprisoned soldier, they still
believed that England was the land of liberty.
Politicians from hustings and hall declaimed to
the crowd, that freedom was an Englishman's
birthright; and although the jails were full,
although any man might be deprived of his
liberty on the mere affidavit of a creditor,
although poor debtors languished and died in
prison, the crowd believed the statement, and
shouted the parrot-cry back in triumph. As for
the penal code, it was simply murderous; and in
reading of it now, although we marvel at the
number slain by the gallows, we marvel more
how any man, being poor, suspected, and accused,
could escape the hangman's hands. Such escape
would have been rare indeed, but for that natural
sympathy with the criminal, which is the inevi-
table result of sanguinary laws.

It was to this sympathy—exaggerated in her
case—that Maurice attributed Madeline's un-
willingness to yield up Mr. Rathline's accomplice
to justice. That the hawker was his accomplice
he never doubted, and that he was now willing
to sell his friend, if he could do so with safety
to himself, he never doubted either. And being

resolved to bring the bargain to a successful
conclusion, he was careful, in his visits to
Madeline, not to mention Mr. Rathline, or in
any way arouse her suspicions concerning him.
He therefore avoided all allusion to the subject,
which they had discussed so angrily on the day
of her arrival.   This made their interviews all
the pleasanter, although it could not take from
the hearts of either the painful, secret conviction
of a silent antagonism.   Madeline, however, on
her part, was glad of this rest.   It seemed like a
few days' truce between two battles, for she could
not blind herself to the fact, that she and
Maurice were at issue on a point, where neither
would give way an inch, and the day of warfare
between them must come sooner or later.

Here in London, with the hard, practical
world all around her, Madeline confessed to herself that the course she had taken appeared too
romantic, too generous, too daring even—for
how could she presume to ignore laws and
customs, and pass sentence singly on that careless, selfish culprit?—but down in Cornwall, by
the wild sea, with solitary heath and hill spread
around her, and one careworn, sorrow-stricken
face pleading silently for life and pity, the path
she had followed seemed the only one possible;
and the lenient sentence to which Lord Crehylls
had himself consented, was the mildest justice,
and the sole form of justice, to which her heart

could agree. If Maurice would only understand that she was right, and generously leave her unquestioned, how relieved and thankful she would be! But Maurice had no thought of this; he was only gathering his forces for a harder battle.

In those days the post was so slow—though that generation considered it fast—that Maurice had been obliged to consent to Madeline's lonely stay at the hotel, as he could scarcely expect his letter would recall his mother back from Hastings under a week. Great was his surprise, then, when a note reached him, saying she was at home, and wished to see him instantly. The messenger bringing this had followed him to the inn, where he was paying his daily visit to Madeline. He read out the news joyfully.

" Let me call a coach, and go with me at once to Harley Street," he said. " It irritates me to see you here, Madeline, so lonely and unprotected."

" I am quite safe," she answered; " and before going to your mother's, I think I had better wait for an invitation."

She had remarked that the letter contained none; Maurice had not observed this.

" Are you so ceremonious?" he asked, with a vexed air. " Well, I'll go at once, and bring my mother to fetch you in an hour."

He bent over her, and kissed her. Madeline took the kiss a little coldly, a little proudly. A

whisper in her own heart told her, that Mrs.
Pellew's sudden return, could not mean hospitality and kindness to her.   Gradually, day by
day, there crept upon her the conviction, that
the forlorn Miss Sherborne was not so welcome
a guest as Miss Sylvester, of Penkivel; and she
did not hope to find Maurice's worldly family
more generous than others.

*   *   *   *   *

Mrs. Pellew rushed forward to meet her son,
with an open letter in her hand.   She looked
excited and weary, full of fuss and amazement.

"Read this!" she cried.   "Your father sent
me up to town directly I received it.   I got it
the same day I had yours.   As to returning to
London, Maurice, that is quite impossible at
present; and I suppose you'll hardly wish it
when you have read this."

She put the letter in his hand, and sat down,
fanning herself excitedly.   The letter was from
Lady Crehylls, and Maurice read it with a haste,
terror, and indignation, indescribable.

"My dear Mrs. Pellew," she wrote, "it is
my painful duty to apprise you of my sorrow,
else, Heaven knows, I would willingly keep
silent.   But it is right your son should know,
that the woman to whom he has given his affection is utterly unworthy of him.   She has

alienated my husband's heart from me, and not content with making me feel her influence in daily unkindness and coldness, she has now persuaded him to leave his home for ever. This he acknowledged to me himself, in a parting and cruel interview, wherein he confessed that her power over him was so great, that he quitted me for ever in obedience to her wish. I am too wretched, too distracted, to enter more fully into details. I am bereaved both of husband and child. My beautiful boy is lost! Whether Madeline Sylvester has stolen him from motives of revenge, and love of power, I know not; or whether he be dead—murdered—I cannot say. My days and nights have passed in an anguish beyond words to tell. But I do not write to speak of my sorrow or of myself. I simply send you a word of warning. I am aware that Miss Sylvester has gone to London; but her journey is but a *ruse;* she will doubtless meet Lord Crehylls at some appointed place; therefore, be on your guard against her protestations of innocence, supposing she dares to make them.

"A report is spread in this county that my husband was on board the revenue cutter, which is gone down with all hands on board. I take no heed of this story, not even to contradict it. I know it to be utterly without foundation. I know from my husband's own lips, that he left me at Madeline Sylvester's commands. I tell you this only for your own sake, and implore you, by all you hold dear, to keep this sorrowful fact a secret. Let me spare my husband's name. Give me this sad satisfaction; it is all I can do for him now. He will come back to me one day and thank me.

" Far and near, the rich and the poor alike are searching the country for my darling boy; and I pass every hour of the miserable day in an alternate fever of hope and despair. As if this were not enough to crush me, my dear father lies hopelessly ill. The day after that terrible girl quitted my house, I happen to know a letter was brought to him from her by Grace Chagwynne, an old servant of the Crehylls family. This agitated him most fearfully; but he would not speak of the circumstance to me, and he even denied having heard from her. Then the loss of the child being made known to him, his illness increased greatly, till at last, while conversing on business with some stranger, foolishly admitted to his room, he fell senseless, and has remained so ever since.

" Whether I am mad or sane I scarcely know. I am stupefied by grief; my faculties are mercifully benumbed, otherwise I believe heart and brain would both give way. I have sent a message to Oxford for Mr. Crehylls, my husband's brother. I shall put everything into his hands. I feel unfit for worldly cares. The

great cry of my soul is for my child. Let me
only have my boy restored to me, and I will go
back to Penkivel with him and my stricken
father, and there try to hide my broken heart
from the world.

"My dear friend, do me one kindness. If
your son sees that cruel woman, tell him to
entreat her to be satisfied with having wrecked
my peace; tell him to implore her to give me back
my child. If she will show me this mercy,
I will try to forgive her. I will promise even
that I will not molest her, but I will trust to
God only to bring me back in time the heart of
my poor, lost Geoffrey. In full reliance on your
sympathy and your silence, I am, dear Mrs. Pellew,
your distracted friend,

"AGATHA CREHYLLS.

"P.S. If Madeline Sylvester will take money,
offer her money,—any sum she pleases, in return
for my child."

"There! what do you think of that?" cried
Mrs. Pellew, as her son, with trembling hands
and ashy face, laid the letter on the table before
him.

"I think Lady Crehylls is mad," he said,
slowly. "The loss of her child has turned her
brain. I have seen Madeline every day since she
came to London. She is as innocent as you
or I."

"Is not her coming to London a suspicious circumstance?" returned Mrs. Pellew. "She may be lingering here a few days only to blind you."

"Mother!" exclaimed Maurice.

"My dear," replied his mother, "a little indigtation on your part is not surprising; but depend on it, you throw it away. Lady Crehylls would never have written that letter unless it was true."

Maurice gazed at her in a silence full of doubt and agony; his mental faculties for the moment were overwhelmed, and he had not the power to form a sentence.

"I may as well tell you now frankly," continued the fashionable and worldly Mrs. Pellew, "that your father and I consider it, on the whole, fortunate that you are freed from this unlucky engagement. We were unwilling to quarrel with you on account of it, but an alliance with a Sherborne would have ruined you."

"Mother," said Maurice, in a hoarse voice, "you liked Madeline once. You invited her here always; it is your fault if I loved her."

"My dear boy," responded Mrs. Pellew, quite unabashed, "Miss Sylvester, the daughter of a rich Indian nabob, the ward of Mr. Lanyon, of Penkivel, was a person worth cultivating. I am not responsible for her being an impostor. I never thought she would turn out to be the daughter of such a dreadful creature as Walter Sherborne. I object to her on account of the highly disagreeable story connected with that name; I object to her still more as an impostor; and I object to her most of all as a disreputable young woman who ——"

She stopped, for Maurice had started up, and held his hand towards her, imploring silence.

" You need not be so violent, Maurice," she continued, in an aggrieved voice, as her fan went more hurriedly than ever. " I object to violence; it is ungentlemanly, especially when shown by a son to his mother; and I have full warrant for what I say. Here is Lady Crehylls' statement; and if that is not enough, here is your own."

" Mine?" exclaimed her son.

" Yes, yours," she replied. " You wrote and told me she had flung off Mr. Lanyon's protection, and was here in London at an inn, without means, and positively alone. Alone!—a girl of her age!—and receiving your visits, I suppose. It is positively disgusting. And do you believe any woman in her senses would thrust herself out of house, and home—being penniless, too— unless she had something to fall back upon? In a word, are you so blind as to believe she would quit Mr. Lanyon, and all her chances of a good portion, unless she was half crazed by love for

Lord Crchylls, and knew at all events that he
would take care of her?"

Mrs. Pellew asked the question with withering scorn; but her son did not answer her.   He
seized his hat, and rushed from the house like a
man out of his mind with some sudden and desperate sorrow.

CHAPTER XI.

WHEN Maurice reached the street he called a coach, and flung himself into it. His first impulse was to seek Madeline; but as he drove towards the inn his mood changed. The whole story was incredible,—a mad, blind, foolish fit of jealousy on the part of Lady Crehylls; and he would not insult Madeline by a single question or doubt. Then suddenly he remembered, with a fierce throb of the heart, that Mr. Rathline had insolently said something of the same kind; so he instantly resolved he would go to him and demand an explanation. In the whirlwind of his fury and his pain, Maurice thought of grappling with the swaggerer with a sensation of relief. He could say nothing to Lady Crehylls, and with his mother he must bear patiently; but he could wreak his indignation upon this low slanderer, and force him either to retract his words, or else to relate truly the substance of what he had heard at Crehylls. So the horses' heads were turned towards Chancery-lane, and very soon Maurice alighted at one of those dens in Cursitor-street, appropriately termed sponging-houses.

"I wish to see Mr. Rathline," he said, in a quick, sharp, voice, when the chained door was at last unlocked, and a grimy individual, of a sallow aspect, opened it just sufficiently to show his own suspicious countenance.

"Mr. Rathline!" exclaimed the yellow face; "now, don't thay, my dear thir, that you are come with newth of another detainer—now don't thay that."

"I have no intention of saying it," returned Maurice. "I want to see him, that is all."

"Well, I'm glad it'th no worthe," observed the grimy man, putting a thick finger by the side of his hooked nose in a leering, and cunning way; "becauth I wath afraid you might be a creditor; and in that cathe it would be a loth to you and me, you thee."

"I don't see," replied Maurice. "Will you let me pass? I am in a hurry."

"Then you are a creditor!" cried the man, opening the door a little wider in his excitement. "Oh dear! what a pity you didn't come a little thooner; Mr. Rathline wath bailed out an hour ago, and all the feeth paid."

The news made Maurice stagger.

"Where is he gone?" he cried, eagerly.

The man put his finger on his nose again.

"Where ith he gone?" he said. "Ah! it

ain't likely he'll let uth know where he'th gone,
—not if he can help it, you underthtand. But
there, you go and lodge your affidavy, and
give uth the writ and I think we'll find him.
That'th our buthineth, you know, to find
people."

"Who were Mr. Rathline's bail?" asked
Maurice.

"Well," said the man, "he wath a reth-
pectable man, a tharp-faced man, called Whalley.
He wath the rethponthible party, you thee. The
other wath a regular bailer—one of the fellows
hanging about the court, you know, who would
bail Old Nick for five thillings."

Baffled and angry with himself at the false
feeling of security which had made him delay his
interview with Mr. Rathline, Maurice asked a few
other eager questions, but could elicit nothing to
give him a clue to the swaggerer's haunts.

"To think such a fellow should have a friend!"
he said, angrily. "I never expected he'd get
bail. Who is this Mr. Whalley?"

"A country party," said the bailiff,—"a green,
I expect."

"No doubt of that," returned Maurice. "He'll
be hunting for this scamp by-and-by, to make
him surrender to his bail. When you have him
let me know, and I'll pay you well. Or, if you
will find him for me at once, I'll pay you better."

"Get your writ, then, my dear, and we'll find

him," remarked the grimy man, with great confidence.

"Unfortunately, I can't take that advice,"
said Maurice; "Mr. Rathline owes me nothing."

The yellow individual's countenance fell con-
siderably, and it was evident his interest in
Maurice decreased instantly.

"That'th a pity," he answered. "But if you
want him very particular, you might get your
writ all the thame. An affidavy can be managed
—ther'th plenty will be glad to do it for a
pound."

At this mild suggestion of forgery, Maurice
shook his head, and retreated to his coach.

"Well," observed the grimy individual, following him, anxiously, "make it ten pound, and
we'll nab him. Only you thee, with a writ, our
fellowth do it profethionally, with more heart;
you can't expect without a writ to have it done
tho quick, or tho well."

"For ten pounds, I shall expect Mr. Rathline
to be found in a week," returned Maurice, as he
got into the coach. "Bring him to this address
when you get him."

He put his card into the Jew's hand, and
drove off.

"Now, vy didn't I ask him twenty pound?"
cried that Hebrew, remorsefully, as he closed the
door behind his own yellow countenance, and so
vanished within his den.

The disappointment he had just met with in Mr. Rathline's escape added a tongue of fire to the burning of jealousy, anger, and doubt in Maurice Pellew's mind. The shade of coldness in Madeline's manner, her obstinate refusal to give him her confidence respecting her discovery or pretended discovery of the Carbis mystery, her firm resolve never to return to Penkivel, her confession that Lady Crehylls had commanded her to leave the castle, rushed upon his memory now, like so many proofs of guilt, till there seemed to blaze up in his heart a great pile of evidence, before which his love shrank and perished.

"Are you come for me?" said Madeline, advancing to the door to meet him. "I see you have brought a coach. I suppose your mother was too tired to come with you? Oh! I shall be so glad to find myself safe under her care."

She looked agitated—even frightened; but Maurice, overwhelmed by his own emotion, did did not perceive hers.

"Madeline," he exclaimed, "I am nearly bereft of sense and reason. My mother refuses to receive you—refuses even to see you; she accuses you of a fearful crime. She dares to say you have destroyed the happiness of Lady Crehylls for ever."

Gazing at him, with the colour slowly fading from her face, but with the shadow of a cold resolve hardening every line, Madeline listened to this in perfect silence.

"Have you nothing to say?" he cried, madly. "Speak, Madeline, if you have any heart or pity!"

"What can I say?" she replied, proudly. "Do you expect me to go upon my knees to entreat your mother to be gracious to me? I warned you long ago that as a Sherborne I should be despised."

"Are you fencing with me?" said Maurice, suppressing his passion by an intense effort of will. "This accusation respecting Lord Crehylls —answer that, Madeline, I implore you."

"I cannot answer it," she returned, calmly.

"You cannot?" he cried.

"No; I cannot," she replied; "or, rather, let me speak the truth bravely, I will not. If Lady Crehylls is unhappy, the fault is her husband's, not mine."

This reply entered the ears of Maurice Pellew, stabbing his heart as it came. Had a pistol been in his hand, he might have shot the girl who spoke to him thus, while she, utterly unconscious of his jealousy, gazed at him in innocent wonder and fear.

"Am I to understand," he said, with white lips, "that this is the only answer you intend to give me?"

Madeline was trembling now. The battle she

had dreaded was pressing hotly upon her, before she had gathered her forces to meet it; the hand she held towards her lover shook and quivered—so did her voice, when she spoke softly.

"I can tell you nothing more, Maurice—nothing. Trust me, or let us part."

"It is easy for a heartless woman to talk of parting," said Maurice, beside himself with the anguish of jealousy and scorn. "As to trusting you, it seems mine has been a fool's trust—a blind, mad, idiot trust,—and I am punished as I deserved to be. Like father, like daughter. There is rakish blood in you, Miss Sherborne."

At this dreadful insult Madeline started to her feet, with cheeks on fire and eyes blazing, but not a word came from her parched throat. She felt choking, and the room seemed on fire.

"Why did I love a Sherborne?" continued Maurice, trembling with rage. "Would to Heaven I had never seen your fair, false face!"

"You are insulting me like a coward," said Madeline, scornfully; "but I deserve it. I might have known a worldly man like you, would soon repent of your rash love, for a girl whose very name is a reproach. Yet I am not ashamed of being a Sherborne, Mr. Pellew; and I will keep my name. You are free—you have always been free. There was no need of a quarrel to cancel our foolish engagement."

She walked towards the door, but Maurice stood before her, barring the way.

"If a woman can interpret a man ungenerously, she never loses an opportunity of doing so," he said, bitterly. "Madeline, answer me one question. Has Lord Crehylls quitted his home at your desire?"

They stood face to face; he, white and trembling; she, pale and resolute.

"If I say yes," she answered, "what then? It can alter nothing between us."

"But do you say it?" he cried, fiercely. "Do you say yes?"

Madeline bowed her head in assent. She was marble white now, and her eyes were bent on the ground; she could not look on Maurice Pellew's face, and part with him. There was a moment's silence; her confession had struck him dumb with agony and rage.

"Maurice," she said, in a low tone, "I foresaw this breach between us, yet I could not stop in the course I had resolved on. I told Lord Crehylls this would part you and me for ever. But I had hoped to part friends. I did not expect insult and contempt."

"You told Lord Crehylls that this would part us," he exclaimed, in intense anger. "It was very unnecessary information, Miss Sherborne, I

·should think. And as for the friendliness you expected from me, I cannot see your claim to it."

"Then neither can I," she answered, sorrowfully. " Let me pass. Why should we prolong this terrible scene ?"

But to prolong its torture is the very thing jealousy demands; so Maurice had no thought of permitting her to leave him thus.

" Stop !" he cried, wildly. " I entreat you to reflect before you persist in this dreadful course."

" It is too late to reflect," she replied, as she wrung her hands together tightly. " I counted the cost long ago. I know what I do, and what I have done."

"Great Heavens !" cried Maurice. " Then Lord Crehylls is a villain ! — a despicable, cowardly villain !"

Madeline was silent. The thought of all that she had lost to spare this careless man the degradation of the law shook her soul, and for a moment her resolve tottered before her anguish. The next instant Maurice himself had strengthened it.

" I say he is a villain," he continued; " but still, his wife loves him. Think, Miss Sherborne, of the crime you commit when you separate man and wife. Turn back for Lady Crehylls' sake, if not for your own."

" Is Lady Crehylls always to be considered ?"

returned Madeline, indignantly, "and myself never? Is the wrong Lord Crehylls does his wife so great, or so terrible as the many wrongs he has done to me? You plead foolishly when you plead for that pampered and spoiled idol, Agatha Crehylls. I have no sympathy to give her—positively none."

"Are you so infatuated?" cried Maurice, as he struck his forehead with his clenched hand. "Are you so hard, so cruel, so lost? And will you let me ask you one bitter question, Miss Sherborne? What was your love for me worth, that not one softening, or pure thought interposed to hold you back from this desperate path?"

"My love for you!" echoed Madeline, mournfully. "How could I dare cling to it, knowing as I do that your thoughts are not my thoughts, and that what I do you would deem a madness?"

Maurice looked up at the pale, pure, marble face of the speaker, and dashed his hand across his brow again in utter bewilderment.

"Am I in my senses?" he said to himself. "Is this Madeline to whom I am addressing such language?" Then he utterly broke down, and his face fell upon his clasped hands. "Madeline," he said, "I would never have believed this, except from your own lips. And even now, I entreat you to pause. Parted as we are for ever, I still implore you to have mercy upon yourself. Give this woman back her husband, and restore to your own heart a portion of its lost peace."

"I leave Lady Crehylls her father," replied Madeline, with a return of coldness in her voice. Then she broke out, bitterly, "Did they leave me my father? Did they ever show me any mercy? Have I been spared one pang, or one agony from my miserable childhood even to this day? I told you there was a blight and a mildew on me. You see the fruit of it now. I tell you I hate Agatha Crehylls; and if there is one spark of joy in the burden of woe I bear, it is the thought that she will be made to feel some slight portion of the pain heaped upon me."

The gloom, the pride, the impulsive vehemence of her nature burst forth in this speech, crushing down Maurice's last hope of saving her. When he spoke again, his tone was hard, even contemptuous, for her avowal of hatred to Lady Crehylls sounded to him like a confession of love for her husband.

"Your words are vindictive," he said; "and if you really feel them, I see she can hope for no pity from you. But you might have left her her child."

"Her child!" exclaimed Madeline.

"Yes, her child!" replied Maurice. "And she offers you money—any sum you choose to name—for the restoration of her boy."

"Do you know what you are saying to me?" asked Madeline, with ashen lips. "If your love for me was a lie—a poor miserable sham, lasting only while the sun shone, you need not tear the veil from my eyes with insult."

Once more the practical man, who knew the world, gazed with passing doubt into the face of the girl, who knew nothing except the romance of her own gloomy life.

"Is the offer of money such an insult to you?" he said, dubiously. "Then restore the child out of womanly pity, if you have any. As for reference to my affection, I pass it over. After outraging it as you have done, the taunt that I only loved you while the sun shone is not worth a reply." ·

"Perhaps not," she answered. "I was foolish to reproach you. The loss of such a heart as yours is no real grief. In a little while I shall be glad that it is gone. What is love without trust? Tell Agatha Crehylls—for I see now you are her messenger—that I know nothing of her child."

With all her old calm, wrapping her almost like an icy mantle, Madeline bowed to Maurice Pellew and pointed to the door. But her coldness only added fuel to the blazing fire of his wrath.

"I shall not leave you until you have heard all I have to say," he cried. "In spite of your cruelty and your treachery, I can pity you still, for you are but a girl—a child—ignorant of the gulf into which you fling yourself."

"Mr. Pellew, I have had enough of this," interposed Madeline. "I do not need your pity."

"Henceforth," he continued, like a torrent, "when you and I meet, I shall pass over on the other side; but now, at least, I will tell you the truth. Miss Sherborne, just now I likened you to your father. No, it is your mother you resemble—that fair, treacherous woman, who brought strife and bitterness beneath every roof she entered."

At these cruel words a deathly paleness spread over Madeline's face, but she still retained her composure, and she still kept her gaze, half disdainful, half mournful, fixed on her mistaken lover. Twice now she had seen jealousy, and failed to recognise it. And if she did not perceive or comprehend the meek, weeping jealousy of a woman, it was scarcely possible she would understand the raging, scornful, contemptuous jealousy of a man.

"You have not stolen the child from his mother, you say," resumed Maurice, steadying his lips to speak sarcastically, "you content yourself with taking the husband. May I ask, when and where you meet Lord Crehylls, Miss Sherborne?"

"Nowhere," she said, with blank amazement and innocent wonder in her eyes. "Why should I give myself that pain?"

A rush of blood flew to the face of Maurice Pellew, making him stagger like a drunken man, yet he would not believe his eye-sight, he believed only his jealousy, and the voice of his mother.

"You cannot deceive me," he replied, bitterly. "I wonder you try to do so. Of what use is it now?"

Madeline heard his voice, but not clearly. A strange bewilderment had fallen on her mind—a doubt, a horror, at which she dared not look.

"Do we comprehend each other?" she said, with her steady eyes fixed upon his scornful face. "Do you know the truth, Mr. Pellew?"

"Too well," he answered; "and mark me, you will live to be a world's wonder,—a byword of contempt,—a thing which no honest man or woman will name, and my curse will be with you!" he cried, as his voice rose in jealous madness. "There is not a safe spot upon this earth for you and that villain. My vengeance will find you wheresoever you hide; and I'll shoot him down, even in your arms."

It was spoken now, and coarsely; and as she rose before him, all the horror, all the indignation and contempt, all the unutterable loathing of her heart, flashed into her eyes.

A foolish woman is pleased at making her lover jealous; but even then it must be the jealousy of the spirit,—the jealousy that thinketh no evil; but a proud woman can never forgive the terrible insult to her honour and her truth, implied by that fierce jealousy, whose passionate breath degrades and humiliates her soul.

"Mr. Pellew," said Madeline, "your thoughts of me are worthy of you,—yes, they are worthy of the man, who can insult an unhappy and friendless girl, through the misfortunes of the dead. You have touched my father and my mother with a slanderous tongue. I will never forgive that. No, not while I have a breath of life in me! You have insulted me like a coward, because you know that throughout the whole wide world, there lives not a single hand to lift itself in my defence. Yet I might pardon that, if my forgiveness did not mean a contempt past words—if it did not mean that your suspicion degrades you so deeply in my estimation, that I can never think of you again without shame. You have said words to me which a woman can never repeat, and never forget."

Here the whole expression of her face changed suddenly, the cold, rigid lines broke into scornful mirth, and a ringing laugh burst from her lips.

"So you think Lord Crehylls has eloped?" she cried, "and with me! You think we love each other, do you?—we two. And we are to meet in some fool's paradise, where sin does not turn to suffering and hate. Oh, this is too much—too much!"

Her laugh rang through the room again as she spoke. There are times when we laugh unwillingly, yet feel compelled to give way to the emotion, through nervousness, through the incongruous ideas presented to the mind, or through a half-pity for the blindness of our opponent. Thus, as Madeline thought of the true and terrible relations between herself and Lord Crehylls, a grim sense of humour seized her—a humour that had nevertheless something in it dreadful and repugnant, and with this was mingled such a passion of scorn for her lover's jealousy, as made her laughter sound like madness in his ears. But even as the echo of this bitter laugh struck her, coming back to her sense of hearing as though not her own, the shadow and the memory of her mother rose before her—the mother whom Lord Crehylls had loved and forsaken. The remembrance added to her indignation against Maurice a sting, and intensity of which, he could never dream. Her cruel laugh died on her lips, and her face paled again to its old marble hue. This return to coldness and calm, mantled too, as she was by her fearless innocence, chilled Maurice Pellew's heart, and chained his tongue. Contending emotions stifled his powers of speech.

One instant he was full of all the agony of remorse, for truth has an accent which never deceives, and Madeline's scornful words and bitter laugh had rung the knell of his jealousy; but the next instant it lived again a wounded life, and he revived it with all the taunting phrases against woman's falsehood, which haunt the tortured souls of the jealous.

"I believe our interview is finished, Mr. Pellew," observed Madeline, icily. "To-morrow I will return you your letters. And these, I think, were yours."

She took a gold locket from her neck, and a ring from her finger, and laid them down close against his hand. There was something small in this; it was one of those little things, infinitely little, which women do even in their sublimest moments, and do wittingly, enjoying the sting they give, and the contrast presented to the mind between the gifts they return and the gifts they revoke. A girl takes her love from a man, and gives him back his trinkets, which perhaps console him. At all events, they only moved Maurice to intensest anger. He swept the shining bits of gold to the ground, and rose up with face white and quivering.

"Madeline," said he, "will you exonerate yourself from this horrible charge? Will you explain your share in the departure of Lord Crehylls from his home?"

" No," she answered. Her voice was steady and unquailing, so were her calm, clear eyes. There was no love or pity in their depths—he had killed these.

" Will you dare to part with me like this,—without a word of explanation ?" he cried.

"Explanation of what ?" she said, looking at him with a sort of calm wonder. " Are you so blinded that you expect me to reply to insult ? The man does not live, who could so make me shame my own soul."

Oh how he had longed to hear her say, " I am innocent ! "—how he had yearned for the indignant and passionate denial, which he had fancied she would be eager to give ! And this calm setting aside of his charge, this cold disdain of it and of him was all that he had gained.

" You will not speak, then ?" he cried, extending his hands towards her in eager passion. " You will give me no answer to take back to my mother ?"

His mother ! At that moment there was not a woman in the whole world, whom Madeline despised as she did Mrs. Pellew. In his hot jealousy and haste he had not told her of Lady Crehylls' letter ; he had mentioned her only vaguely, as offering money for her boy ; so to Madeline, his mother appeared as the instigator of all his calumnies.

" I send no message to a slanderer," she said.

"I am weary of all this; I think you might spare me the pain of your presence now."

"My mother is no slanderer!" cried the angry lover. "She had warrant for what she said; and if you will deny nothing, and explain nothing, how can I do other than believe her?"

"Believe what you will, Mr. Pellew, only spare me further insult," returned Madeline. "I am tired of it. Your mother has succeeded; we are parted; let that suffice."

She had reached the door and passed into the hall before Maurice could stay her exit; and, swelling with pride and anger, he stood silently gazing after her as she went slowly up the inn staircase.

CHAPTER XII

A S Lord Crehylls rowed towards the *Penkivel*, a gleam of hope broke upon him. He would go secretly to London, he thought, and seek out the first counsel of the day; he would lay before them, under other names, a true narrative of the terrible circumstances surrounding him, and he would ascertain their opinion as to the course of conduct he ought to pursue; he would find out from this whether there existed for him a loophole of escape. But this resolve was destined never to be fulfilled. The storm which raged in the Channel that night swept the *Penkivel* out to sea, and all other thoughts, for a time, were swallowed up in the sense of the fearful danger that threatened them. On reaching the schooner the sea was already so rough, that it was found impossible to send a boat ashore with the child. Reluctantly, therefore, Lord Crehylls saw himself obliged to take his boy with him. He hoped, however, the storm would lull

before morning, when he trusted to relieve the
anxiety of his wife by restoring the child. But
the gale rushed across the Bay of Biscay, and
drove the schooner before it down to the shores
of Spain. Thus much time was expended; and
when fair weather came at last, other dangers
threatened the *Penkivel*; indeed, in this time of
war, a ship was safer in storm than in calm.
Running the gauntlet of French privateers, from
which the *Penkivel* escaped by her fleetness, she
nevertheless had to double and twist so often,
with such consequent loss of time, that, in the
end, it was two months before Lord Crehylls
found himself safely landed at Genoa. Thence
he wrote to his wife, and promised to send his
boy home to her by the first safe opportunity
that occurred. By the expressions of grief and
affection breathed through his letter, by his
allusion to events which he supposed her to be
acquainted with, Lady Crehylls, terror-stricken
and amazed, saw dimly that her husband had fled
from some danger of which she knew nothing.
That Madeline's hand had drawn this on him she
felt sure; but not the remotest suspicion of the
truth touched her mind. She could question
no one; her father's mind was quenched in
paralysis, and her husband would speak only in
enigmas. After a silence of many weeks, she
wrote to Mrs. Pellew, confessing that she feared
she had done Madeline an injustice; but her

letter arrived too late to remedy the evil, which
her jealousy had accomplished.

*   *   *   *   *

" You are ill," said Tom Singleton, looking in
Madeline's white face anxiously. " You are
agitated and excited.   What has happened?
Will you tell me, and can I help you? "

" I fear not," returned Madeline, in a sad
voice.   " I do not see how any one can help me."

" Not if you don't tell 'em what is the matter,
of course¦ they can't," observed Alice, in her
rough way.   " But I bet now, Tom will find a
way to help you if you only let him know.   Why,
you are looking exactly as if you had seen a
ghost! "

" I believe I have seen a ghost," replied
Madeline, growing paler as she spoke.   " The
truth is, Mr. Singleton," she said, turning
towards him frankly, " I have reason to fear I
am not safe here, and I wish to go away."

" Not safe! " repeated Tom, in amazement.
" Who has dared to molest you? "

" A man who would dare anything," she
answered.   " I met him first in Italy; he followed me there like a shadow, till I grew to have
a strange terror of him."

" Who and what is he? " asked Tom, with a
flush rising on his face.

" He is a Russian," replied Madeline, " a man

who can speak fluently all the languages of
Europe, and I believe him to be a spy in the pay
of France."

"Then I should uncommonly like to knock
him down," observed Tom, cheerfully. "It
always seems the natural and right thing to do
with regard to spies. And I suppose you have
seen him since your arrival in London, Miss
Sherborne?"

"Yes; I saw him this morning," replied
Madeline. "It seems he followed me from the
Park; and he has now taken rooms in this hotel."

If the blood rose to Madeline's face as she
spoke, and tears sprang to her eyes, it was at
the thought that Maurice and his family had
deserted her at a time, when she most needed
their protection, but the outspoken Alice interpreted her emotion her own way.

"Well, I think you are rather fond of this
lover of yours," she said, "else you wouldn't
blush as you do."

"Miss Sherborne has not said he is a lover,"
remarked Tom, gravely.

"There is more of hatred than of love in his
pursuit of me," said Madeline, with a shudder.
"Mr. Singleton, I hold this man in deadly
abhorrence and fear. I must leave this house.
What shall I do?—where shall I go? I am in
terror of my life while under the same roof with
him."

" Will you come to my mother ? " cried Tom, eagerly. " I'll answer for it you shall not be molested there; not while I have an arm to defend you."

Madeline had journeyed to London with slighting thoughts of Tom Singleton. She had gone to his poor abode meaning to patronise him— meaning magnanimously to share her poor little income with his abject and wretched family, and now she found herself glad to accept the asylum which they offered, and thankful for the protection which he gave her in so simple and manly a way, that it was impossible to interpret it in any other light than its own true and friendly one. The hospitality, which she had hoped to receive from richer, and older friends, was denied her with contumely, and the love on which she had leaned had failed her.

" I thank you very much," she said to Tom Singleton, in a faltering tone, as she held out her hand to him. " I will trust to your kindness gladly."

" Hurrah ! " cried Alice. " Then I vote we carry her off at once, Tom, while she is in the mind, and before this French dragon swallows her up alive."

" Will you come at once, Miss Sherborne ? " asked Tom, a little timidly.

" Oh yes, this instant !" exclaimed Madeline,

" if you will. My enemy is away now, so we shall go unwatched."

Affairs in Tom Singleton's hands did not take long to settle, and it was surprising how soon everything was arranged, and they were rolling along in the coach to their destination. It stopped, not in the shabby suburb, at the mean row of houses, but at a bright little dwelling with a pretty garden in front; and Madeline was led, bewildered, into a gay, sunny room, which Tom Singleton told her was her own.

" Now you see how hard he has been working since you came to London," said Alice, in triumph.

" Why did you do this?" asked Madeline, reproachfully.

" I did it for you," returned Tom, quite simply.

" But the money?" cried Madeline.

" Don't trouble yourself about that," said Tom Singleton. " I really got it so easily, that I am quite ashamed of myself for having remained poor so long. It appears that a man of my expectancies can find friends if he will."

Tom closed the door as he said this, and left Madeline and Alice by themselves. He seemed afraid of thanks.

" Now don't make a mistake about his expectancies," cried Alice. " I hate anybody to misunderstand Tom. He don't mean, that he

10—2

thinks you'll ever condescend to marry a quiet, good little fellow like him; he means only, what he'll have when poor mother dies. He never borrowed any money before, because mother hated the thought, and he said he should feel like a heathen if he did it against her will. We had fine trouble to persuade her to it now, I can tell you. Some folks, you know, if they are ever so sickly, don't like the idea of money being got which is to be paid back when they die. However, we persuaded her through father; we said if we moved he'd never find us out again, and then, with a good cry, she gave in. You see Tom wouldn't borrow on a ' post-orbit' —that's what they call it—without asking her leave. Ah! if there is another man in the world like Tom you find him for me, and see if I don't marry him, that's all. I don't like your showy men much. Father was a showy man. He was a good deal to look at; he was some-thing like Mr. Pellew now——he's showy too, he's good in sunshine, but if I'm out in a storm, give me Tom."

With this remark Alice took her departure, first informing Madeline she was going to her domestic duties, and checking off on her fingers sundry items of hard work, which nothing less than a female elephant in the shape of a maid of all work could possibly get through.

" Good in sunshine," repeated Madeline, when

she was left alone; "but if I am out in a storm——" She stopped suddenly, and glanced round the pretty but unfamiliar room, the unknown haven she had found in danger and sorrow, then her bitterness found vent in tears, and Maurice Pellew's name trembled on her lips unwillingly. Perhaps, in these last sad moments of her love, her sorest thought was that she had cut herself adrift from him for ever.

*   *   *   *   *   *

"So Miss Sylvester, or Sherborne, or whatever her name may be, has vanished!" said Mrs. Pellew to her son. "Of course you were prepared for that, were you not?"

"No," said Maurice, abruptly, his face all aflame with anger. "Mother, what a Job's comforter you are!"

"Not prepared for it?" returned Mrs. Pellew. "And yet Lady Crehylls' letter was explicit enough. What other conclusion to the affair did you expect? Lord Crehylls having vanished, of course Miss Sherborne vanishes likewise. She did not leave her address, I suppose, at the inn?"

"No," replied Maurice, shortly. "Mother, do not speak of Madeline to me. I cannot bear it."

He rose and quitted the room. He feared his mother would question him, and he was unwilling to acknowledge that, having vainly

sought Madeline in London, he was now resolved
on travelling into Cornwall, in the forlorn hope
of hearing something of her from Mr. Lanyon.
But without a question his mother guessed his
determination, and secretly rejoiced at it, as it
enabled her to fulfil a plan of her own.   Ever
since Madeline's history had been confided to
her by her son, she had chafed at his engagement,
and she caught eagerly at this opportunity of
breaking it.   The lovers were parted now, and
she was resolved they should not meet again.
While she talked to Maurice of Madeline's disappearance, she knew perfectly well that she
was with the Singletons, for a letter from Tom,
giving their address, was then actually in her
possession.   It was therefore with great satisfaction that she heard Maurice say he was going a
journey, and should be absent fully ten days.
He would not discover Madeline in Cornwall,
but there was a chance that he might if he
remained in London ; hence it was very consoling
to know that he was going so far in a wrong
direction.

Meanwhile Madeline was learning to know
Tom Singleton.   She was brought into contact
daily with a nature so gentle, refined, and generous, so nobly, patiently brave and good, that he
brought to all those who loved him a sense of
trust, repose, and happiness indescribable.   Who-
ever once loved Tom Singleton, loved him for

ever. No friend he had ever forsook him or
forgot him.

After the first few days of her sojourn, Madeline discovered that her hosts were still exceedingly poor. The sum Tom had borrowed had
been expended in furniture, and in the expenses
of removal; and when the little balance was
gone, it was hard work indeed to make the poor
clerk's salary support so large a household.
Madeline saw, too, with vexation, that her
room was furnished with luxuries not to be
found in the other rooms; and a thousand little
artifices were resorted to in order to hide their
poverty, and increase her comforts, without permitting her to see the cost at which this was
done.

When she had been his mother's guest about
a fortnight, Tom returned home one evening
from his work, with a strange expression on his
face, half joy, half sorrow.

"How glad I am to bring you this!" he said,
placing a letter in Madeline's hand. "I have
been expecting to receive it every day."

The letter was in Mrs. Pellew's handwriting,
and Madeline took it with a rush of colour rising
to her brow.

"How did you get this?" she said, eagerly.

"It was sent to the bank, under cover to me,"
replied Tom. "I thought when you came here
you would like your friends to know where you

were, and I fancied, perhaps foolishly, that you felt some little delicacy in telling them yourself of the step you had taken. So I ventured to write to Mrs. Pellew, and explain, that my mother's address being a secret, was not in accordance with any wish or desire of yours, but merely a necessary precaution for our own sakes—alluding, of course, to Mr. Rathline—and—and, in fact, I told Mr. Pellew I should be glad to see him, and I hoped he would call. You see I was sure you wished it, although you have not said a word."

A crimson glow set Tom's kindly face alight as he finished this speech, and yet there was a quiver in his voice, which seemed to tell that Mr. Pellew's anticipated visit would bring to him more pain than pleasure.

"How good and kind you are!" cried Madeline, with sudden fervour. But Tom hated thanks, and even as she spoke he vanished. So she was left alone with her letter, and her heart beat passionately as she broke the seal. Maurice surely had repented of his cruel insults and slanders, and had written to excuse and account for his madness. No! here was only a short note from Mrs. Pellew, and this was couched in terms so insolent, that Madeline read it twice before her mind took in the sense, or could believe that such words as the following were addressed to her:—

"MADAM,—I write by my son's request to inform you, that your very obliging act in forwarding him your address through your cousin, is an unnecessary trouble on your part. Your engagement with my son being cancelled, he considers it would only give him and yourself pain to continue on friendly terms; he wishes, therefore, the parting to be final and complete. So much from him. From myself and my husband, I beg to say that I do not desire to hold any further communication with a person, whose conduct from childhood has been reprehensible and treacherous in the extreme. I can never forget that, even as a child, your deceit was so deliberate, that for years you sought and received my kindness under a false name, and, under false pretences. Your powers of deception are very great, and I am not surprised they have culminated in an act so treacherous and cruel, that, to give it a name, would stain my pen. Perhaps, also, I ought not to wonder that, after separating a husband and wife, you should still deem it necessary to feign affection for my son; but I confess I am amazed at this, and can only suppose you do so to further some scheme of your own, of which I am ignorant. I trust you will spare me and mine, the pain of any further attempt on your part, to heal a breach which your own conduct has made imperative and eternal."

With this letter lying at her feet, Madeline sat in silence an hour. In this short time a thousand good and generous feelings, ever springing up in her soul among all the weeds sown by pride, secrecy, and gloom, perished. All the daily groping struggles towards the light which had chastened her passionate, morbid nature, sank down and died. Henceforth the blight and the mildew, of which she had so often spoken, were to be triumphant. A bitter, rankling sense of injustice, done to her by every human being with whom she had been brought in contact, filled her soul as with a deadly venom. She had been cheated out of gratitude and affection; she had been cheated out of love. In all relations of life, to her, all things had proved a failure. Mr. Lanyon's kindness sprang only from the meanest motives of self-preservation; Maurice Pellew's love was a broken reed, which had pierced her the moment she leaned on it for help.

Oh, how she repented of the weakness which had made her listen to him at Crehylls! She was right, at first, when she refused him; she was right in the instinct which told her the world held no happiness for her; she was right in feeling that upon the whole earth there beat no human heart, which could ever give her its entire love and trust. And the greatest sting in Mrs. Pellew's cruel words was the truth in them.

Deception, dishonour, and treachery, had indeed surrounded her all her life long ; these sins were not hers ; but the blight, and the blame, and the suffering, had been heaped on her unjustly ; and now, love, hope, and happiness were wrecked.

When Alice and Tom came back, entering the room with lights, they found Madeline lying on the floor, with face pale and cold, and the letter held tightly in her clenched hand.

CHAPTER XIII.

THE NARRATIVE OF ALICE RATHLINE.

I AM asked to tell my share of this story. I expect I shall make a queer jumble of it, for I am not one of your clever ones,—by no means; and as to romance, there is no more of that in me than there is in a pair of bellows; and, like them, I'm good enough for blowing the fire; but you must not expect me to keep an organ going too. In fact, with a pen in my hand, I feel like a pig with a silver fork, —I don't know what to do with it. However, since my manuscript is going to be touched up by somebody who can spell, and who knows where those little horrid stops ought to come in, I suppose it will read out pretty straight in the end. So now for a beginning.

From the day that Tom brought Madeline a letter from those stuck up Pellews, we noticed a change in her. She grew colder and prouder, and more silent. It was easy enough to see she was miserable, but she wouldn't tell it. She

hardened herself like iron against her grief, she
never gave way to it, or shed a tear that I saw.
All day she worked at her needle, frightening
mother into fits pretty nearly, by the lovely
things she made out of her bits of silk ; and by
night I heard her walking up and down her room
like a creature in a cage. But she didn't get
ill with all this. Bless you, no ; she had the
health and the courage of a lion all the time.
But it wasn't pleasant, for all that. It used to
make my flesh creep to see her white face bending over her work, proud, and silent, and scornful, as some of those stone faces I have seen
since in Italy. It would have done her good to
cry, but she didn't want to do herself any good.
She wanted to nurse her own bitterness, and contempt, and hatred, till they grew strong as fire
in her, and she did it. Cry, indeed ! It is my
belief she would have dashed her head against a
wall, rather than let a single tear drop from her
proud eyes. And all this while I was so sorry for
Tom. Oh, I was so sorry ! Because I saw he
loved her with all his good, kind heart, and she
was not half good enough for him. There, I say
it again, not half good enough—no, nor a quarter.
How could she be, when she was always nursing
her own grief and thinking of herself, while he
was ever caring for the grief of others, and never
thinking of himself at all ?

Oh, Tom, my dear, good, darling brother Tom, I

am a rough girl, with no more schooling in me than
a horn-book could teach in a winter day to a fool,
but I've sense enough to know how good you
were.   I had sense even then to love you, and
eyes to see how true, and faithful, and tender you
were ; and how grieved, dear Tom, how grieved,
when you saw her grieving so scornfully for the
lover, that had forsaken her.   For we understood
it all, Tom and I; we saw Mr. Pellew never
came, never wrote, never cared for her, any more
than if she were dead and buried out of his sight.
And we guessed the letter he sent her was a cruel,
hard farewell.   Oh, the mean, miserable man!
I should like to see myself fretting for such an
animal.   I'd box my own ears till they blazed,
and ten thousand candles danced hornpipes before my eyes.   That's what I'd do; but she hadn't
got sense to give it to herself like that, so she
grew sadder and paler every day, and Tom would
look at her white face till his heart, and his eyes
were heavy with woe.

"Shall I go to Mr. Pellew ?" he said to me. "I
can't bear to see her like this. Shall I go to him ?"

"He isn't a cripple," I answered, "or a fool,
or a baby. He can come to our house, if he
chooses ; and if he don't choose, let him stay
away. If you went to him, you would seem
like her messenger; and if he should laugh at
you, as he most likely would, she would never
forgive you."

Then Tom asked the same question of mother, and she said, for certain it was all over between the lovers, since they neither wrote to nor saw each other, and Tom's interference would gall Madeline, and make her bitter against him too. So we left things alone, and pretended we didn't know, that she was passing through a great sea of sorrow.

At last, one evening, when we were sitting silent by the window, she broke out into singing suddenly. Oh, such a voice! such a wonderful voice! that it made me cry as I listened to her, and Tom held in his breath to catch every note. This was the first time I had heard her sing, and I have never forgotten it. She sang often to us after this, smiling a little sometimes when she saw how silent, and entranced we were. She grew better from that evening; but I think, too, she grew harder and colder, and more bitter against those, whose injustice she fancied had blighted all her life. But Tom didn't see this; and if the poor fellow had given her his heart before he heard that marvellous voice of hers, you can fancy how the magic and charm of her singing drew away his very soul. She didn't know it. I'll do her that justice. She had not a thought of making Tom like her. Perhaps she was too proud to suppose he would presume to love her, and lay down, at her regardless feet, his great, good heart, and his gentle, worthy life.

Well, while all this romance was going on, poor Tom's bit of money was melting away fast. First there was our removal, then debts to pay of father's before we could remove in quiet; then new furniture to get, and all this took a pretty slice out of the sum Tom had borrowed. Then, too, we had to live comfortably now Madeline was with us, and keep a servant, who was a perfect tyrant, with an appetite like a wild beast. So it is no wonder Tom's purse was soon drained dry.

"I must borrow again," he said, quite cheerfully. But at this, mother burst into tears, and said she knew we all wished her dead, else her son wouldn't want to borrow, in the hope of her being put under the ground. So for a good while nothing more was said, but our dinners got very small, and I was obliged to tell a hundred fibs a day to keep Madeline from seeing how we lived. But she found out. For one day, the door being open, our domestic wolf flopped the dish on the table, and bawled out, " Well, if you were four half-penny dolls, you might dine off that bit of meat; but since you ain't, I can't see how you are going to fill yourselves, unless you take to the sawdust like the dolls does."

I had carried Madeline a chop, and had told her some dreadful fib to make her take it in her own room; but now I was sure she would never

believe me again, if she had heard this.   And so
it turned out.   She came to Tom and me that
evening, after mother was gone to bed, and said
quite fiercely, " I am not going to stay in this
house.   I wont be made an idol of any longer."

" An idol ! " said Tom.   And I could hear his
poor heart beating against his side like a ham-
mer.

Oh, my poor dear Tom, I wish I had taken
you in my arms then, and comforted you, and
warned you !   She was a cruel, unloving woman,
her heart closed up in bitterness, rankling with
its own sorrows, nursing revenge and hatred, and
with none of that gentle wisdom in it, which
would have poured out love upon you, and
reaped its reward in happiness.

" An idol ! " cried Tom.

" Yes, an idol," she said angrily, " and one of
the lowest sort ; an idol who has meats and
drinks laid before her, which others want ; an
idol who gets service paid her by feeble hands
and willing hearts, when she ought to work herself.   You are degrading me in my own eyes.   I
feel baser than the dust I walk on.   I wont
bear it ! "

" What will you do ? " asked Tom, sorrowfully.

" I can sing—I'll go on the stage," she said.

" Oh, not that ! " cried Tom.   " Don't say
you'll do that.   Think, with your beauty, what
a mark you will be for evil tongues, and how the

world will deny that you have honour, innocence, or truth !"

"They deny me those already," she said, scornfully. "Even those I love malign me. What the world says can matter little now."

Nevertheless, Tom dissuaded her from the scheme, and it was agreed she was to give lessons in singing instead. But this led to a strange catastrophe. That bad man, who is still the terror of our lives, heard her singing, as she gave a lesson to a little girl living in our neighbour-hood. He was prowling about there, searching for us; and as her voice poured into the street, he recognised those rare notes, and he followed her home cautiously. From that day commenced a terrible persecution. He heaped letters, pre-sents, and threats upon her. One day he wept and implored, the next he raved and menaced. An able, cunning man, but furious and wicked as a madman—a dangerous man, unscrupulous and wary, venomous and deceitful as a serpent, passionate and yet cool—a man to fear greatly, because, in spite of the strength of his intel-lect, there is madness in his veins; there is a twist in his plotting brain which peers out at times in his cunning eyes, when he glares on Madeline, with all the rage of his disappointed love blazing in them. She went in deadly fear of him, I could see that; so I was not surprised when she told us she was certain he would kill her : and tormented by him as she was daily, her hours were a terror and a torture to her, and she was resolved to leave London.

"Stay here, and let me protect you," said Tom, with a shaking lip.

I knew what those words of his meant, but she didn't.

"You can't protect me from a madman," she answered. "He has sworn that he will kill me! He'll keep his oath. I must go away,—and for that, I want money. Mr. Singleton, I laughed once when you said, 'Propose to me, and I will reject you.' But I don't laugh now. I will utter the absurdity,—it is but a slight effort, after all,—and then I will demand the little income my aunt left me. Mr. Singleton, will you be my husband ? Now quickly say 'No,' and let us get it over."

Her eyes were bent upon her work. She never looked at Tom. He wasn't worth a look of hers, you know; but my eyes were fixed upon his face, and I saw it was white as snow.

"But I cannot say it," he answered her, in a very low voice. "I cannot—it is impossible."

"Impossible!" she echoed, glancing at him angrily. "And why is it impossible ? "

"Because—because," faltered Tom. "Oh Madeline ! you will not care to know why."

She gazed at him in an amazed way, her work lying on her lap, and her face getting hard and pale. " I care for nothing," she said. " You need not tell me why, if it pains you. I can give up all hope of my aunt's legacy. I can stay in England and die. What does it matter ?"

" Tom rose and stood by her side, his trembling hand leaning on her chair.

" Madeline," said he, " you have said words to me which, uttered carelessly, indifferently, as you uttered them, stung me to the heart. Yet I cannot say no to them. I say yes. I can only say yes, because I love you with all my soul.'

She was pale now—pale as death, and she glanced up at him with shining eyes full of tears, yet she never spoke a word.

" I cannot reject you, Madeline," continued Tom, his dear kind voice trembling as he spoke; " that would be impossible. But since you really need so much this small annuity now kept from you, I can let you reject me, if you will. And I will try to bear it bravely. Madeline, I once said, ' I will not propose to you, because I do not love you, and I cannot ask you to be my wife for the sake of money.' Well, that scruple exists no more. I love you dearly, and I can ask you, with an honest and true heart, to fulfil the conditions of my aunt's will. Don't mistake me," he added, eagerly, as her head drooped ; " I do not say this in hope. I say it, knowing full well what your answer will

be. I say it, because I cannot belie my own
heart by letting the rejection come from me.
No, it must be yours, Madeline, only yours.
And when you receive this little income, and
you leave us, as you say you will, remember
always, that while you stayed you made me very
happy by your presence. And—and may God
bless you, Madeline."

I cannot tell how it happened, but Tom had
seized her hand in both his, and dropped it, and
was gone, before I could utter a syllable. As for
Madeline, she sat where he had left her, with her
head drooping forward on her hands, and I heard
her murmur softly, "Always the noblest—always
generous, where I am mean—always noble where
I am base."

"So you are finding out Tom at last," I said
to her, crossly. I was obliged to speak crossly,
else I should have cried.

"Are you here, Alice?" she answered, half
laughing.

"I am always here," I returned. "There is
nothing going on that I don't know it. Tom
didn't mind speaking before me."

"I don't think he would mind speaking
before the whole world," said Madeline, rising
wearily. "He is not ashamed of his love, or
of me."

"Well, you see, his gloves and his boots are
not quite so dandy as Mr. Pellew's," I said,

mischievously. "And a good deal depends upon a man's boots. Mr. Pellew's Hessians are a little too fine for our parlour."

    *   *   *   *   *

"Madeline," said Tom the next evening, mother being gone to bed as usual, "have you written to Mr. Brydges?"

Her face grew red, then white, but she said "No," quite steadily.

"Why do you delay?" asked Tom, "and this madman pestering you daily."

"Why should I write to Mr. Brydges?" she asked.

"To demand your legacy," said Tom, "the conditions now being fulfilled."

"Are they?" she answered. "Did I say 'No,' when you asked me to be your wife? I don't remember it."

"Madeline," cried Tom, coming over to her side, and leaning over her, breathless, "what do you mean. Tell me quickly."

"I mean that I cannot take advantage of your generosity," she said, calmly. "My aunt has done you a great injustice in her will; why should I perpetuate it? Let us share this money."

"The hundred a year," asked Tom, faltering more and more.

"No, I mean the whole fortune," she said,

holding out her hand to him, in the same cold, calm way. "You are a good man, and you love me,—that I truly believe. Take me if you will."

Tom did not touch her hand.

"Not for the sake of money," he said, sorrowfully. "Surely you do not accept me for the sake of the money? I cannot buy you, Madeline. Unless you come to me with a willing heart, Heaven forbid that I should selfishly yield to the weakness of my own. It is cruel to tempt me with your hand, not loving me."

He took her hand in his as he spoke, then laid it softly down and turned away. In my eyes he seemed then a very king for dignity, and truth, and honour.

"Tom," said Madeline, in her softest voice, "you are worthy of the noblest love a woman can give, but I have none to offer you. I come to you bitter, angry, and forsaken. Yet let me say this: if I had to choose this moment between you and the man who, like a coward, has deserted me and insulted me in my distress, I would choose you. To you I give my whole esteem—to him I give my contempt, and the dregs of a love that I despise."

"Ah, Madeline, you speak in anger," said Tom. But he came back to her, and looked wistfully into her eyes.

"I speak deliberately," she answered.

" But you love him still," continued Tom (he had her hand in his now), " and married to me, you would be unhappy and full of regret."

" I am not so weak as to cherish love for a man who has calumniated and forsaken me," she said, answering the first question only.

" That's pride again," I muttered to myself. " I wish she would think of Tom a little more, and of her own feelings a little less." But his great love bewildered and blinded him, and mistaking her answer, he fancied she surely loved him a little, else she would not of her own accord accept his big true heart. So he put his arm around her, and would have kissed her, but she drew back, and laid both her hands upon his shoulder.

" I have something to tell you first," she said. " I have a confession to make to you."

Then she turned her eyes on me, as much as to say, " Go, if you please, Miss Alice." But I held my ground.

" If you put me out of the room," I said, " I shall listen at the door ; and if I can't hear then, I shall go round to the window. I warned you I was the most curious girl alive."

" It matters very little," she observed, as Tom ordered me to go—" let her stay. Perhaps she had better hear it. I wish you to know that, in taking me, you do not ally yourself with so guilty a name as you think. I

know, for a surety, that my father was an innocent man ; I know it as certainly as I know who
the real culprit is."

Tom seemed startled and distressed.

"Why speak of this, Madeline?" he asked.
"It is you whom I love. I needed no assurance
of this kind from your lips."

"But for my own sake, for justice' sake, I
desired to tell you," she said.

"Herself again," I grumbled. "The bucket
always comes from the same well."

"And you must never ask me for the proof,"
she continued, her hands still on his shoulders ;
"neither must you demand of me the name of
the person for whose guilt my father perished,—
I have promised never to reveal it. Now tell
me, honestly, can you let me keep this secret,
and not be angry? It is the only one I shall
ever have. All other thoughts of my heart
shall be open to you; but I desire to keep this
secret, not only for my promise' sake,—though I
scorn to break a promise,—but for the sake of
an old man, a dying man, who succoured me
from childhood, and whose love and kindness
have been my shield against the orphan's
fate—cruelty and neglect. Now will you let
me fulfil my duty towards this friend, as
my own conscience tells me I should?—and
will you never interfere with my desire for
silence?"

"Never," returned Tom, solemnly. "Loving you as I do, it would be strange if I could not trust you."

"It is fair I should tell you that Maurice Pellew would not trust me," she said, proudly.

"I am glad he wouldn't," replied Tom, smiling a little; "his want of sense has made me so happy. And, as it appears to me, this affair is entirely your own; if your own conscience tells you that it would be wise, and kind to keep this wretched man's name, and guilt a secret, I see no reason why you should not. It might be gratifying to clear a father's memory, but if you owe a clearer duty to your adopted father, to my mind you do right to fulfil it."

"I was sure you would say so," she answered, quietly. "Yet there is one thing more I must tell you: I am a mark for scandal. Lord Crehylls has quitted his home, never to return, and Mr. Pellew believes me to be the cause. I confess it. I am the cause—the innocent cause —of this exile; and I must ask you to be content with this assertion, and never demand of me a fuller explanation."

"I am content," said Tom, as his kindly face beamed with joy. "What more can I want than your word?"

"Then her hand fell from his shoulder, and turning away, she said, almost in a whisper,

" You shall never repent trusting me, Tom. I will try all my life long to repay you."

She gave herself to him by those words; and feeling this, Tom clasped her in his arms and kissed her. He was bright and radiant, she calm and quiet; and when his lips touched hers, her face was colourless as marble. I noticed, she had never once said she loved him.

That is how they came to marry; and I never liked it from the first. I was downright angry the next day, when she took me aside, and told me what the doctor had said to her about mother. She must go abroad to a warm climate, or she would die.

" So Tom and I will marry at once," she said; " then he will have money to take her."

" If you marry for this, thinking that you do Tom a kindness," I cried, " you are very wicked. Such a deed would cut him to the soul. He would rather die than take you for his wife, if you do not love him."

" You are a child," she answered, coldly. " What do you know of love ?"

" I don't know love, but I know Tom," I returned, " and that is enough. Besides, how can we go abroad amidst all this fighting ?"

However, before that day fortnight, they were married, and we had sailed away from England. Just before we left, there came a letter for her.

She did not know the writing on the address; it was Mr. Pellew's; but so altered through illness, she could not recognise it, and she opened it hastily. Then she saw his name, and called me to her side.

"Come here, Alice," she said, "and see me seal up this letter again. I will not read it. But here is another not his; it is from Lady Crehylls. I keep this. But I will not wrong Tom by reading a single line written by Mr. Pellew."

She said that; but I never saw a woman weep as she did that night.

*   *   *   *   *

There is not much to tell for two years. Then poor mother, who at first had got better, grew worse, and died. Sick and weakly as mother had ever been, her loss was a great blow to us; for somehow she kept us together as one family. Her death made Tom a rich man, but not a happy one. Madeline had always been a cold wife to him; and now that he was wealthy, and no longer needed her money, which she seemed to think she owed us, she grew colder, showing more than ever that she was not one of us, and often looking, in her weariness, as though our lives were a torture and a madness to her passionate, impulsive nature. And yet, through all her fitful moods—her silence, her coldness, her storms of repentance and sorrow—how Tom loved her, and bore gently with her woe! Always hiding from himself the truth, that, as the years progressed, she grew more moody, more angry with the world and with herself.

About this time my brother Ned gave us trouble. He was bitten by the soldier mania; and though he was but a boy, he was big enough to be killed. And killed he was, poor fellow, by a French bullet. This grieved me so that Tom removed us to Naples for a change. There we stumbled upon father—positively father—alive and comfortable as ever. But that did not surprise me so much, as to see Madeline make a friend of him. Madeline talked confidentially with him, and evidently showed there was a secret between him and her—a secret unknown to Tom. Oh, how she tried that good, kind heart! —how hard she tried it! Sometimes I think I will never forgive her.

Lord Crehylls was at Naples, too, a pale melancholy man, half mad, people said, from long imprisonment in France. Madeline never spoke to him, but they passed each other at times, and he looked strangely at her face, and she at his. He had his son with him—a boy about the age of Alfred, on whom he doted —a pretty fair-haired child; and he and Alfred, who was the life and light of our house, grew to be friends, and played together daily.

I am coming now to the saddest time of all my life, and I must hurry it, no matter how I mar the story in the telling.

Father had some grievance against Lord Cre-hylls,—it was easy to see that.

"The money I have spent to find him," I heard him say one day to Madeline (I was always prying about, I confess that), "and now to be kicked from his door by these lazzaroni of his! I'll not bear it! I'll show him Dick Rathline is a gentleman not to be insulted with impunity! 'Gad! the loss is his, in not seeing me,—not mine. I could tell him something to set his hair on end!"

"You had better be quiet," said Madeline, seeing me listening.

"I think so," I answered. "You had better be quiet, for once and all. I hate such dark-lantern talk!"

Soon after this, being in our garden late one night, I saw Madeline sitting in the balcony alone. In the moonlight her face looked strangely white, and beautiful as a statue's. In a minute she began to sing softly to herself, and from singing she fell to weeping. Then I saw my brother, from the room within, rise, and come to her. I could hear their voices plainly, and I listened to them. I always listened when I could. I am of a mighty prying disposition, and always try to hear all I can.

" Madeline," said Tom, " if all the love that I have given you cannot win love back—if my presence pains you, and kind words only vex you to tears—let us part."

" Part ! " she said, in a strange voice ; " part ! Would you leave me ? I should be wretched then, indeed."

Her face fell down upon her hands, and I heard her sob bitterly.

" Do I mistake you, Madeline ? " said her husband. " I long only for your happiness ; for that I could break my own heart, and leave it. Why should I persecute you with my love, when it is only a weariness to you ? "

" Tom, dear Tom," she cried, with arms thrown suddenly about his neck, " it is not so. You mistake me, indeed ! I am not worthy of your love. I am full of bitterness and hatred. I cannot be happy ! There are memories which rankle in my mind ; there has been a blight over me from childhood. I am writhing always beneath a great injustice. Shall I never, never be revenged ?"

" My dear love," said Tom, soothingly, " let us be happier together, and leave vengeance to Him to whom it belongeth."

" You are always good," she murmured ; " you are a thousand times better than I. Without you I should sink—sink down into the wicked woman that I am. And yet you love me?" she added, as if in wonder.

I could not hear Tom's answer, but Madeline's next words came upon my ear distinctly, ringing passionately through the night air.

"If God had given me a child, I should have found peace. Agatha Crehylls has a son—I am childless!"

"Is Alfred not like a son to us?" asked Tom, cheerfully. "I look on him as our own. He is a splendid boy."

She did not heed his words.

"Agatha Crehylls," she repeated, "the woman for whose happiness my life was crushed—for whom, lest a breath of sorrow should touch her, I was made to lie and hide my name,—she has a child."

"But you confess you have sent her husband from her," urged Tom, gently. "And I have kept my promise, and never asked the cause."

"Yes," she said, "it is true her husband is an exile, but her child will soon be with her. He goes back to England in a week. To think of her joy burns my heart up. Through her I lost my father, and my friend Mr. Lanyon, and my lover—the poor, false man! If through her I ever incur another loss, let her look to it, for the chain holding the evil down within me will snap like threads."

"Hush!" interposed Tom. "You talk wildly,

Madeline. Morbid thought has warped your nature. Do not fear that Lady Crehylls will be too happy when her boy returns. Remember, her father is dead, and her husband and she are parted for ever. I am sorry the boy goes; Alfred will lose his playfellow."

"And Agatha Crehylls will regain her child. I wish the boy would die," she said bitterly, "that she might never see his face again."

"Are you so envious?" asked Tom. Then he bent over her pitifully, saying, in the words of Elkanah, "Do not grieve, Madeline, that we are childless. Am I not more to thee than ten sons?"

With his arm around her he drew her within the window; and soon I heard her voice sweeping gloriously out into the night, singing to him the English air, "Home, sweet Home."

*　　*　　*　　*　　*

It was the next day it happened. Father came rushing up the garden with a wild, white face, and clutched me by the arm, trying to put his shaking lips together to speak; then failing, —then trying again, and forcing the words in a hoarse whisper :—

"Tom is dead!—drowned! Prepare her for the shock. They are bringing him home. I hear the feet of the bearers."

With that he rushed away again breathless, while I uttered a shriek that went up to the blue sky. When I turned, Madeline was by my side.

"What is it?" she said, in a frightful whisper. "Who is dead?"

My face told her; and as I saw hers slowly whitening, I fell senseless.

When I awoke, it seemed a dream, and I could not weep for a long, long while.

Oh, Tom! my dear, good, kind brother, may God bless you for all your love!—the love that went out so freely from your generous heart to all who needed it—to the poor, the sorrowful, and the sinful. Oh Heavens! what a sad world this is, where the just perish, and the wicked flourish!

I think I was ill for a week or longer, and quite wandering in my mind. I remember I heard the doctor say, it would be good to make me shed tears. Then Madeline came to my bedside in widow's weeds. She looked like a woman frantic with grief—her face snow-white, her eyes fierce and dry—and leaning over me, she whispered, "Alice! Alice! why are you so hard? Have you no tears to give your brother? Oh, Alice, I never loved him as I ought. I never loved him with all my heart till now—now that he is dead, and I have rained down unheeded tears and kisses on his cold face."

Her burst of grief appalled me, but it did not make me weep. Then some one standing by, told me the story slowly—how Lord Crehylls' servant was in a boat on the bay with his master's child and little Alfred; and father and Tom, in another boat near by, saw him shift the sail unskilfully; and in a moment all were in the water. Instantly Tom plunged into the sea, and saved his little brother, then diving, he clutched the other child, but as he lifted him, the drowning servant seized him by the arm, and all three sank to rise no more.

" Your hear this, Alice," interposed Madeline; " he died striving to save the boy Crehylls! They have not found the child's body, but they have brought my husband home, and I have buried him. And the night before—only the night before—I promised him I would be happier, and love him better."

She cast her arms about me passionately, and my tears gushed forth at last. As I grew better, I missed little Alfred's merry voice, and asked for him.

" Do you think I could bear the sight of his face ?" said Madeline. " I have sent him away for a while, till I can endure to see him, and yet remember how Tom died."

Shortly after this, I found Alfred was in my father's hands, and when I wrote for him, I had a surly letter, refusing to give him up. " The child is mine," he wrote, " and I shall keep him. You have no right to him, nor Madeline either.

12—2

So let me hear no complaints because an affectionate parent is resolved to take care of his own son."

I was full of anger and wonder, but the wonder ceased when I heard of Tom's will. In it he left all his property to little Alfred, on condition that he took the name of Singleton. He appointed Madeline his guardian, and said that, by her own request, she having already enough, he bequeathed her no legacy except this infant brother, whom he implored her to love for his sake. To me he left two thousand pounds, saying Madeline had promised to make me her especial care. This was his will, and it accounted to me fully for father's new affection for his boy. I looked to Madeline, as his guardian, to do her duty, and save the child from his evil hands, but to my surprise and horror she refused, declaring no one was so fitting as a father to have his son. Upon this I quarrelled with her, and strove to find the poor child myself. I failed in every effort, and soon discovered that father had gone away with him, none knew whither. During my search, I went to see Lord Crehylls. His mind was quite shaken by his loss, his wits seemed nearly gone; they wandered each moment to some dim time and events, of which I knew nothing. One instant he told me to thank my brother for striving to save his child, the next he would remember he was drowned, and beg my pardon pitifully. As for himself, he was an unfortunate man, he said, suffering for a rash deed done in youth, but he hoped soon to be at rest.

"The day," he murmured, "is nearly over,—that short day of mistakes, errors, and remorse, which we call life."

He seemed a weak man,—indolent, unready, infirm of purpose; but my heart bled for him, and I wished him farewell, with tears.

Angry with Madeline's cruelty to Alfred, I quitted her, and went for two years to a convent school. When I emerged into the world again, I heard that she was famous. A great singer, a great actress, her restless heart had at length found the fame and the adulation it ever craved.

This is all I have to tell, except that I have never seen father, or my brother Alfred, since the day Tom was drowned at Naples.

CHAPTER XIV

ON a dreary November evening, when a cold mist lingered in the air, and the watery sky hung grey, and low on the wintry landscape, a carriage drew up near a lonely church, and a lady habited in mourning alighted. Bidding the servants await her return, she crossed the ancient stile leading into the churchyard, and, with faltering step, hurried towards a new granite tomb, shaped like an obelisk, which stood coldly white and glittering in the pale sun. As she approached it, two figures rose suddenly from among the gravestones, and stood before her. One was our easy friend, Mr. Rathline; the other was a child—a fair boy, with delicate features and golden hair.

"Lady Crehylls, I presume," observed Mr. Rathline, raising his hat.

Lady Crehylls bowed to him silently, wondering much at his easy insolence, and looking round, half in fear, to ascertain if her servants were in sight.

"Madam," said Mr. Rathline, assuming what

he thought to be the manner of a gentleman, "you have nothing to fear. I have the honour to be a friend of the late Lord Crehylls."

"Indeed!" said the young widow, with quivering lips. "May I ask where you knew my husband?"

"Well, madam, I—that is to say, I ought to have known him at Genoa, five years ago," stammered the swaggerer; "but, unfortunately for me and himself, he got into some trouble for want of a passport; the upshot of which was, that in trying to get on into the interior, he came in contact with the authorities, and, ultimately falling into the hands of the French, he was detained as a prisoner for three years."

"Well, sir," said Lady Crehylls, with a heavy sigh.

"Well, madam, owing to these untoward events, I missed him at Genoa, which, I assure you, was a great loss to me and to himself; then at last, hearing he had escaped, and was at Naples—a place protected by the English fleet—I hurried thither, and had the pleasure at once of making his acquaintance."

"What was your business with him?" asked Lady Crehylls, coldly.

"Really," answered Mr. Rathline, "I could not well explain just at present; but if your ladyship will grant me a private interview, I shall be happy to communicate some information of importance to yourself and family."

"Family!" repeated Lady Crehylls, mournfully. "Sir, I stand alone in the world; you should apply to the present Lord Crehylls, if your business is connected with his family."

She walked on, as though she considered him dismissed; but, with all his easy impudence rampant in him, he coolly followed her.

"I think your ladyship will one day be sorry if you do not grant me an audience," he said, with a cunning smile. "Or, if you choose to listen now to a word or two ——"

Lady Crehylls glanced around her on the darkening church, and sombre yew trees, with some trepidation.

"Not here," she said, hurriedly; "and not now—it is impossible."

Mr. Rathline took off his hat, with an assumption of respect and sorrow which sat very ill on him.

"Madam," said he, "I am aware this is a sad time for you. I had the pleasure of seeing my friend Lord Crehylls immediately after the accident, which deprived him of his boy, and I assure you his affliction was extreme —so extreme that he was quite unfit for business, and I was forced to defer an important conference."

"Did you ever see my boy, sir?" said Lady

Crehylls, turning towards him suddenly, with eager eyes.

" Often, madam," was the reply.

" And was he changed ?" she asked, feverishly, " or was his face the same as when I saw it last ? Ah ! I forget," she added, clasping her hands together wildly, " you never saw him at Crehylls. You cannot tell what he was like then."

" He was a pretty boy—a lovely boy," answered Mr. ●athline. " Alfred," said he to the child beside him, " stand back, sir. You are in the lady's path. And I am sure," he continued, " your ladyship is aware that his loss preyed so deeply on the mind of Lord Crehylls, that it aggravated his malady and hastened his death."

Lady Crehylls bent her head in assent. She seemed too moved to speak.

" I think your ladyship also knows, that during his lordship's long detention in France, his greatest sorrow arose from the fact, that he found it impracticable to restore the boy to his mother. It was impossible to send so young a child on such a difficult journey, especially as he must have been intrusted to strangers."

" Sir, I have heard this from my husband," returned Lady Crehylls, " yet he never mentioned to me the cause of his sudden departure from England ; and if you can enlighten me on that point, I shall be glad to see you to-morrow at Penkivel."

"Madam, I believe I can clear up that mystery," said Mr. Rathline, with a smile of satisfaction. "I will certainly do myself the pleasure of waiting on you; the more especially as the subject you have broached is the one on which I wish to speak."

Lady Crehylls looked at Mr. Rathline with curiosity, and then her eyes fell wistfully on the boy standing timidly by his side.

"Is he yours?" she said, suddenly.

"My youngest," returned Mr. Rathline. "A fine boy, madam."

"Yes," she answered, with a deep sigh. "I think he must be the same age as Aubrey."

"A little older," said Mr. Rathline, "but not so tall. Your lad, madam, was a tall boy for his age."

The bereaved mother's eyes filled with tears, and, stooping, she kissed the little Alfred, and laid her hand upon his head tenderly.

"He was Master Aubrey's playmate," continued Mr. Rathline; "they were inseparable, those two."

Lady Crehylls started as she heard this news, and her fair face grew hectic with a painful flush.

"His playfellow?" she cried; "my boy's? And he has seen him, kissed him, been his little

friend—been loving and kind to him, perhaps.
Oh, this is too much—to think that I should see
a child who has played with my child ! "

Her tears fell like rain, and, kneeling on the
pathway, she put both her arms around the boy,
and looked him earnestly in the face.

" Oh that I had your eyes," she said ; " they
have seen the face of my child. Tell me, can
you remember him ? did you love him, my dear?
Will you try to tell me what he was like ? Did
he resemble me ?"

" I remember the little boy I used to play
with," replied Alfred. " No, he was not like
you. I was very sorry when he was drowned—
I cried all day for sorrow."

As Lady Crehylls heard this she sobbed
aloud, and kissed the child again. It was the
strangest, saddest thing to her to see a little one,
who had played with her boy, and loved him,
and wept for him when he died. She looked
into Alfred's eyes greedily, longingly, and held
his small hand with a mother's touch.

" Sir, if you had told me at first that your
child and mine were playmates, I would have
held out my hand to you at once," she said,
in a trembling voice. " Your boy shall never
want a friend, while I live—remember that, sir,
always." Then holding both hands of the child,
who looked upon her earnestly, she said, in a
grave tone, " My dear, I want you to feel always

that I am your friend; and, if you need help
you must come to me for it, and you shall never
come in vain.   I am Lady Crehylls—do not
forget my name; and when you think of me—
as I hope you will sometimes—remember that
I love you for my lost boy's sake."

Lady Crehylls then rose from her knees,
tearful and very pale.

"Sir," said she to Mr. Rathline, " I shall
·expect you to-morrow at Penkivel; and I trust
you will kindly bring your little boy with you."

"With pleasure," returned Mr. Rathline.

Had Mr. Rathline been a gentleman, he
would have left her now, but he lingered till
she drew so near her husband's tomb that in
very shame he was compelled to quit the churchyard, and leave the lady to her lonely sorrow.
Then she knelt down on the granite steps, and
in the fading light she read dimly the mournful
words, which recorded the titles and virtues of
Geoffrey, Lord Crehylls, who died at Naples, in
the thirty-sixth year of his age.

CHAPTER XV.

SEVEN years have passed since we last saw Maurice Pellew, and he is still a bachelor. He sits now alone in his dull chambers, sorting dusty papers. Among these he finds a packet headed "Rathline," and he tears it open with an eager hand. It contains only a short correspondence between himself, and that lively young Hebrew, who had undertaken, for a consideration, to find this easy gentleman. The last letter of the list concludes thus :—

" The debt and costs for which Rathline was arrested have been paid by a London solicitor, employed, we believe, by Whalley. This last is hunting for Rathline himself, doubtless to recover his money ; but the search will be as useless as ours. Rathline left England a fortnight ago, in a vessel bound for Genoa. This is certain,—the fact admits of no doubt."

Maurice put down the letter, and took from his desk his own private journal.

"Genoa," he said, thoughtfully. "And I remember it was at Genoa, that poor Lord Crehylls first landed, when he left home in that strange mad way, seven years ago."

Turning back the leaves of his journal, Maurice then perused these entries :—

September 28th.—I have received a letter from Lady Crehylls. She has heard from her husband. He is at Genoa; his boy is with him. She confesses, that whatever may be the motive which induced Lord Crehylls to take this extraordinary voyage, it is not the one she supposed. Thus ends her cruel aspersion of Madeline. And yet, Lady Crehylls still persists it was Madeline, who insisted on her husband's departure. I could learn nothing, during my visit to Castle Crehylls, to elucidate the mystery of this occurrence. All my efforts to discover Madeline have failed. My mother assures me that not a single line or message has reached her. Is Madeline so unforgiving?

September 30th.—I have been to the banker who employed Mr. Singleton. He has resigned his situation. They do not know his private address. A fellow-clerk remembers his speaking of having removed. He has never made any mention of Madeline. Can she have taken refuge with the Singletons? Anxiety totally unfits me for work. I was mad to listen to the jealous ravings of a weak woman like Lady Crehylls. I deserve this torture for my folly.

October 4th.—Another letter from Lady Crehylls. Madeline is not at Penkivel. I had nursed a forlorn hope that she might have returned thither. Lady Crehylls, being fully satisfied by her husband's letter that Madeline is not with him, expresses contrition now for the hasty judgment she had formed. But her repentance comes too late; it only irritates me, accompanied as it is by the persistent declaration that it was at Madeline's desire that her husband left Crehylls. It is utterly useless to question Mr. Lanyon; paralysis has rendered him childish, and his daughter says he is sinking fast.

Michael Polgrain is not to be found; he is hiding from the search made for him by the preventive service men; so it is evident I must for the present give up the hope of discovering anything through him. Lady Crehylls is still ignorant of Madeline's true name. My mother has kept the promise she made me, not to divulge it; and, knowing what was the wish of Lord Crehylls on this subject, I have not considered myself justified in revealing Madeline's parentage to his wife. Hence she speaks of her as Miss Sylvester, and evidently regards her (most unjustly) with feelings of distrust and dislike.

October 6th.—I begin to feel much alarmed.

In every quarter where I have inquired for Madeline, I discover I have been frustrated in my questions by a foreigner, a thin, dark man, very eager in his inquiries, and lavish in his offer of bribes. I find this man was at the same inn with Madeline, and the servants say she showed fear of him. She particularly requested he might not be informed of her departure. What can be the meaning of this? Did I quarrel with her at the very moment she most needed a protecting arm?

October 7th.—I hear from a friend that Mr. Singleton borrowed three hundred pounds on a post-obit bond, just after the period of Madeline's arrival in London. I am convinced now she is with the Singletons. The young man must have got this sum, in order to give her the comforts, not procurable by his small income. I will write to Mr. Brydges, of Lymington.

October 8th.—The foreigner is a Russian—a spy in the French service, but, in reality, a double traitor, for he is well paid both by his own Government and by France. I heard this in confidence from one whose name I will not set down even here. He is considered very adroit in his profession of spy, perfectly unscrupulous, and fearless and skilful. "Worth all the money paid him," my informant said. Can this be the lover of whom Madeline expressed fear to me on that memorable morning when I walked with her to St. Eglon's Hut? If so, then Mr. Singleton stepped in to her aid at a time when she needed help, and I—idiot that I was—forsook her like a coward.

October 9th.—I have received the strangest letter from Lord Crehylls, stating a supposed case, and asking for counsel's opinion on it. Great Heavens! can it be of himself he speaks? If so, then I understand his sudden departure from Crehylls at Madeline's command. I understand her refusal to divulge to me the discovery she had made of the Carbis mystery. I perceive how natural it was Lady Crehylls should grow jealous, being ignorant of the true reason of Madeline's power. In fact, I comprehend fully the pain, and mystery, and anger of the last three months. Oh what a madman I have been! I grow fevered with my vain search for Madeline. But I must and will find her.

October 10th.—A note from Mr. Brydges. He will not give Mr. Singleton's address without that gentleman's consent. He has written for it. I shall know the result in a few days. How can I wait so long? I am not well. The fever of my mind has brought on fever of body. A constant pain and giddiness in the head warns me of coming illness. I must take rest.

Same day.—Counsel's opinion on Lord C.'s supposed case arrived. It is very unfavourable.

Advises the homicide not to surrender to take his trial—the circumstance of his having quitted England by sea, on the day of the man's death, being fatal. The fact of another gentleman having been tried and condemned for his offence would also be so damaging to his character, that the minds both of judge and jury would be prejudiced against him : counsel thinks he would be condemned ; recommends him to remain abroad and keep quiet. The innocent party having committed suicide, the evil done cannot be remedied ; considers therefore a confession would be unavailing, and certainly ruinous both to himself and family. His estates would be confiscated for his felony, and most likely his life forfeited. If the only person, who has a right to demand his surrender, is satisfied with his exile, counsel considers he should submit to it, as it is certainly a most lenient sentence.

I send this opinion to Lord Crehylls with great regret. I am overwhelmed with horror at the circumstances of this " supposed case." Did that hasty blow kill Carbis, or did the hawker, finding him in the wood wounded, dispatch him ? I incline to the last opinion, and I say Rathline knows the truth, and knows, too, where that villain, the hawker, is. But then again, unless the blow C. dealt killed Carbis, why did Rathline go to Cornwall ? Evidently he meant to

wring money from C.'s fears; evidently he is
gone to Genoa for the same reason. But how
should he know that C. struck Carbis, unless the
hawker told him? This is the great question.
If Rathline is acquainted with a circumstance
known only to C. and Michael Polgrain, who is
his informant? I affirm decidedly the hawker—
decidedly the man who is the true murderer—
the man who finds Carbis stunned and feeble,
and then kills him. If the hawker had seen the
blow struck, and found Carbis dead, he would
either have witnessed to the fact, or throughout
these long years he would have wrung money
incessantly from Lord C. Having done neither
of these things, I come to the conclusion that he
is himself the guilty man. Now for Rathline.
I believe he means to sell this information to
Lord C., or perhaps—which is more likely still—
he intends to tell him he is aware of his supposed guilt, and he will demand money for
secrecy. I shall advise C., as delicately as I
can—so as not to appear to have guessed his
" case "—to give money to no one; and I shall
counsel him, for my own part, to return and
take his trial; and, as I am a living man, I'll
find that villain, the hawker, if he is on the face
of the earth.

It is more than ever requisite I should
see Madeline. I must see her, to lay these
views before her. She has done wrong; she

has acted with a self-reliance on her own judgment most hasty and presumptuous; but she is generous, she will repay her fault. How unfortunate, that at the very time when she and I should consult daily together, with every confidence in each other, we are separated through the interference of that meddling fool Tom Singleton. No—what am I saying? The blame is mine. And how could I speak of hasty judgments after my own rashness? What is Madeline's blindness to mine? Yet Singleton's conduct is maddening. He has no right to hide my affianced wife from me. I'll square accounts with him one day.

October 12th.—If this " supposed case " be really that of Lord Crehylls, I have been wondering how Madeline became acquainted with it. She must have felt quite sure of the truth of her information, or she would not have presumed to pass a sentence of banishment on the unfortunate man she supposed guilty. I am inclined to believe Polgrain was her informant. I know he saw her father just before he died. Perhaps then he made some promise to tell his daughter one day, that he was innocent. Michael looks like a man pursued by remorse. The unhappy Walter Sherborne may have made some appeal to him, which he neglected. My blame of Madeline's rashness is softened. I remember how her father died; and in her eyes Lord Crehylls is his slayer, or at least responsible for his sufferings and death.

How impatient I grow to see Madeline! This estrangement is one long agony to me. I feel more and more bitterly that my conduct was unpardonable. I insulted her horribly, cruelly. I can't think of it; I lose my senses when I do.

I am no better in health. The painful headache and giddiness continue, although I fight strenuously against them. I have made up my mind to see a doctor to-morrow.

October 13th.—At last I have Singleton's address! And now that I have received it, I have not courage to go and see Madeline. The medical man I have consulted says I must keep quiet. How can I, until I have seen her, and we are reconciled? To-day her face haunts me. I fell asleep in my chair, and thought, when I awoke, she was leaning over me, her eyes full of tears of forgiveness and sorrow. I hope the vision is true.

Same day, four o'clock.—I fear I am worse. I ordered a coach to go to the Singletons, and just as I was stepping into it, the giddiness seized me again, and I fell on the pavement. I have sent a messenger to Madeline with a letter, enclosing that terrible one from Lady Crehylls. I have merely said: "Read this. It is the sole excuse I can offer you for my madness. I implore you, let me see you to-morrow, to entreat your forgiveness. I am so ill with anxiety and grief, that this morning, in trying to come to you, I fell insensible; but a kind word from you will give me strength to reach you."

It is strange, but, as they carried me back to my room to-day, I saw Madeline at the door, beckoning. She was very pale, and scornful, and she pointed to her left hand, with a sorrowful smile. Are these sick fancies, or fever?—or, in short, what are they? My thoughts perplex me sorely. I tremble,—I hear the feet of my messenger returning. Is it life or death he brings me?

   *   *   *   *   *   *

" It was very nearly death he brought me," said Maurice, closing his journal, and re-locking it. "I remember, after slow weeks of fever, coming to this desk, and not having strength or courage to open it. I remember through my long delirium how I always saw Madeline by my bedside, with Tom Singleton's ring on her left hand. I can hear again the echo of my own voice in my ears, as I repeated day and night the words of her dreadful letter;—' I will accept no further cruelty at your hands; your letter doubtless contains only calumny and falsehood, so I return it unread. I have had enough of insult from your mother and yourself. Lady Crehylls' letter I retain.

Tell her, if you will, from me, that while we both have breath I will never forgive it, and never forget it. And unless I mistake myself indeed, she shall rue having written that lie to her dying day. My answer to her slander and to yours is this: I am a good man's wife. I am Madeline Singleton.'"

As Maurice finished repeating this softly, he bowed his head upon his hands, and remained a while in silent thought.

"So ended my dream," he said at length, in a bitter tone; "and with it there perished also my ambition and all my aspirations after honour and fame. My life has been a disappointment to myself and others—to none more than to my mother. Of what avail is it that she repents of having separated me from Madeline? The deed is done; our lives are wasted. We two, who should have grown better, being together, have grown worse, being apart. The mildew of hate lies deep on Madeline's soul, and the rust of idleness on mine. I have cared for nothing. I have let Lord Crehylls die in exile, believing himself guilty of a bad man's death, while all the while in my inactive hand has lain the clue to the truth—truth which, I verily think, would have vindicated him, and restored him to his home. So, through my inertion, Lady Crehylls is a widow, her only child is drowned, and the house of Crehylls is without an heir. Heaven!

what a heap of sins lies upon my careless head!
And now, what has roused me to exertion again?
—what has brought to life the old dream of
happiness, the old hope of an honourable career?
The sight of Madeline—only that.   One look on
that wonderful face, so pale, so pure, so perfect,
and I am a boy again, and all those visions throng
around me which love's madness raises.   And yet
not so, for love to the man of thirty-one brings,
not as to the boy, dreams and fancies, but renewed life and energy.   So, once more I am
alive, and being living, I will let slip the dogs on
Richard Rathline."

CHAPTER XVI

THE heat in London was intense,— the pavements were scorching — the roofs glaring in the sun; but in one house, near the Park, a gentle breeze fluttered pleasantly; the venetians of the drawing-room were lowered over open windows and balconies filled with flowers; the polished floors, the white curtains, the soft green of the many-hued foliage in the conservatory beyond, all seemed redolent of coolness.

On a couch, placed beneath the roof of shining leaves, with a pillar on either side, covered with twining plants, framing her like a picture, Madeline Singleton lay sleeping. The deep violet of the robe she wore made the fairness of her face seem wonderful, while the repose breathed around her gave to her transcendant beauty, the quiet and peace it lacked when waking. As she slept, Alice Rathline crept softly in, and stood by her, irresolute. But, quiet as her step had been, Madeline awoke at the sound, and looked up, languidly.

"Why wake me, Alice?" she said, wearily.
"It is such a comfort to sleep and forget."

"I did not want to wake you," said Alice;
"but here is one of your dark lanterns come;
and I thought you would be vexed if we sent him
off."

"Who is he?" asked Madeline, leaning on
her elbow. "Is it your father?"

"No,—he is older and uglier than father, and
seemingly not so easy in his mind," returned Alice.
"Father's conscience, you know, is a charm to
him; he is sweetly at peace always."

"Tell them to send the man up here, Alice;
and you need not stay, my dear," said Madeline,
half smiling, as she looked in her sister-in-law's
face.

"Your secrets are nothing to me," returned
Alice, bluntly, "except when they relate to my
brother Alfred. If the Guy Faux waiting for
you now was father, I'd manage to listen somehow to your talk; but as it is, I shan't trouble
myself."

With this she walked scornfully from the room,
and there entered in another moment a haggard
man, who had evidently once been handsome,
but whose aspect now was so feverish and wolfish,
that the beauty of his features had grown into
hard, rigid lines; and his form was so wonderfully spare that he looked as if the gnawings of
his spirit had eaten the flesh from his bones, and

left him his skeleton, merely that he might have the benefit of his teeth and talons to claw and bite with.

As this individual stood for an instant at the door, he took in with one keen, hawk-like glance all the graceful luxury of the room, the flowers, the statues, the works of art, the costly furniture and draperies of lace, and last of all his piercing gaze fell on the weary, beautiful figure, lying on the couch, framed by the glossy leaves which trailed from pillar and roof.

" Do I speak to Mrs. Singleton ?" he said, in doubt. " My name is Whalley. I am the schoolmaster with whom —— "

" I hope the child is well," interrupted Madeline, eagerly.

This question brought a strange look to Mr. Whalley's sharp face.

" Is he not with you ?" he said, uneasily.

" With me ? No !" she cried ; and starting from her indolence, she seemed suddenly imbued with a new and passionate life.

" Then I grieve to say your ward has left my house," returned the schoolmaster.

" Left ! Who took him ? Who has dared take him from your care ?" she said, in a trembling voice.

Mr. Whalley's lips twitched nervously, as he answered, " No one, madam ; the boy has run away, and I naturally supposed he would come to you."

As Madeline listened to this, she seemed to feel the tidings in every pulse, her lips parted, and her eyes grew fierce and angry.

"You are mad to tell me this," she said. "I gave the boy into your care; I look to you to find him."

"If you don't know where to seek for him, I don't," returned Mr. Whalley, in a hard tone.

"You are the person responsible for the child's safety," retorted Madeline. "I shall require him at your hands. You have treated him unkindly, I presume."

Mr. Whalley seemed speechless with rage at this; he grew to a white heat, and held himself down in his chair with both hands. When his unhappy pupils saw him thus, they had reason to tremble, but Madeline only regarded him with quiet contempt.

"If I have been severe," said he, "the fault is your own, Mrs. Singleton. You desired his father to tell me the boy was unruly, and inflated with pride."

"Did I tell you to torture him into despair and flight?" retorted Madeline. "I wonder, sir, you can dare come here, and tell me that, to escape your cruelty, the child has flung himself on the world."

"The cruelty was yours," replied the irate

Mr. Whalley. " What do you mean, ma'am, by driving the boy to desperation, and then flinging the blame on me? I wont have my school —my respectable school—ruined by such a woman as you—an actress, a singer, who ——"

" Stop," said Mrs. Singleton, holding up her small white hand. " Take care what you say to me. I am not a woman to bear an insult patiently; and I don't want to crush you. I know exactly what your respectability is worth; I know that everything around you is false and hollow indeed."

Mr. Whalley gazed at her in dismay, wondering perhaps why he could not frighten this woman, as he had frightened other women.

" I meant to observe," he said, faltering in his tone, " that your last letter had a great effect on the boy's mind. You spoke of being poor, and declared your determination to bind him apprentice to some low trade. In my opinion, that letter made the child resolve on flight. As to being poor, you certainly have no appearance of it," he added, his light gray eyes wandering superciliously round the room.

" I have a right to luxury while my voice lasts," replied Madeline, a little bitterly. " When that leaves me, the world will let me die in a garret. For the rest, I do not believe a word you say. See here,—look at these letters,—one is from your powerful neighbour, the Earl of

D——; the other from your more powerful landlord, the Earl of F——; and both ask me in what way they can render me a service. Shall I tell them to crush Mr. Whalley, the country schoolmaster?—surely you are almost too easy a prey for such foes—or shall I expose the secrets of your school to the press, and make the papers ring with your cruel name?"

As Mr. Whalley listened to these rapid words, his haggard face grew livid, and he shrunk suddenly into a shivering, abject coward.

"I trust you understand at last," concluded Madeline, "that I have the power to fulfil a threat. And now, perhaps, comprehending your position better, you will deem it wise to confess what bribe you have accepted, and to whom you have sold my ward, Alfred Singleton?"

Her words relieved the schoolmaster of his worst fears; he stood upright again.

"I have not sold him," he answered. "Whom should I find to pay me better than you do?"

His tone, and the terror in his looks, convinced Madeline of his truth.

"Certainly no one," she said, more softly. "Let me know, sir, what measures you have taken to recover the boy."

"Madam," returned the cowed Mr. Whalley, "I rely on your kindness to believe I have had recourse to every means in my power; and after searching far and near in vain, I felt assured he had come hither. Then I took coach and followed, hoping certainly to find him with you."

" He will not come to me," said Madeline, in a low voice. " Have you searched for him on the Cornish—I mean the Plymouth road ?"

"Has he friends there ?" asked Mr. Whalley.

" He has friends nowhere," responded Madeline. " Nevertheless, I believe he has followed that road. Mr. Whalley, he must, he shall be found. I would rather lose my right arm than lose that boy. Go back to the West at once, and search for him in the towns and villages bordering on the road to Crehylls; and if you do not find him, go straight to the Castle and ask for him there."

" Ask Lord Crehylls for him !" exclaimed Mr. Whalley.

" Yes," said Madeline ; " I have often talked to him of the Castle, and the tales I told struck his childish imagination. For what sum shall I draw you a cheque, Mr. Whalley ?"

The sharp, cunning face of the pedagogue brightened at these words, and his eyes glistened greedily. He began to talk of inn bills and coach fares, but Madeline cut him short.

" Understand the child must be found," she said—" never mind at what cost. Name a sum that will find him,—that is all I ask."

Mr. Whalley named a hundred pounds, and pocketed the money with satisfaction lurking at the corners of his thin mouth. As he took the cheque, Madeline glanced at his hands with a shudder. They were peculiar hands—grasping, covetous, avaricious hands—the fingers long and supple, with flattened tips, wonderfully cruel-looking.

"Pray spend no more than this sum, Mr. Whalley, if you can help it," she said, with a covert scorn. "My riches are more seeming than real. A cough makes me a bankrupt, and without my voice, I am a beggar. Remember also that in future, I expect you to render it impossible for my ward to leave your roof."

"This — this happened in the vacation," faltered Mr. Whalley, "and one cannot be always a jailor; but depend on it, in the time to come ——"

"Very well," interrupted Madeline. "The chief point now is to find the boy. Post back to Exeter, and follow the western road till you trace the fugitive. And when you put your hand on him, write to me if any difficulty should arise relative to his return to your house."

"What difficulty can arise?" asked the schoolmaster, with a cruel gleam in his light eyes. "Resistance in a child is nothing."

"But the people with whom he has taken refuge may object to his returning," she replied. "If so, I will go myself and fetch him, or I will send his father. I would accompany you at once, Mr. Whalley, but I am only a slave. My engagements must be fulfilled; I must sing, let my feelings be ever so bitter."

"Madam, your anxiety shall soon be allayed," said Mr. Whalley, rising to depart. "I will send you good news shortly."

"Write to me from Castle Crehylls," she answered. "You will have nothing to tell till you get there."

Mr. Whalley would have held out his hand to her on taking leave, but he checked the movement as he looked upon her ivory face, so strangely bitter, so full of horror, repugnance, and pain; and as the door closed, she fell listlessly on the couch, and shut out the light from her eyes with both hands.

CHAPTER XVII

PLEASE, ma'am, which is the way to Castle Crchylls?"

The voice came from the wayside, from a little dusty, weary figure sitting there, with a small bundle on its fragile arm; and the good dame who was thus accosted started at the sudden question, as she looked down from her high, bony horse on the little speaker. Then her eyes fell on a small, pale child, ill-clad, thin, and sickly-looking, with large, lustrous eyes, and dusky curls clustering round his head. As he gazed upwards into her face patiently, there rested about his little lonely figure an air so wistful and forlorn, yet so brave and gentle, that the good woman's heart was moved with pity.

"The way to Castle Crchylls, my dear?" she said; "why, you are many a long mile from it yet; you can't reach it to-night on foot."

"But I must, ma'am; so will you please tell me the way?"

The childish voice was sweet and pleasant,

but bearing in it a strange ring of pathos, unlike the tones of happy childhood; and good Mrs. Chagwynne, regarding the little tired figure with a perplexed air, proceeded to follow her motherly instincts by asking questions.

"Where do you come from, my dear?" she began.

"From Exeter," answered the boy.

"Exeter!" she cried. "But you have not come by yourself, my dear, I suppose?"

"Yes, I have," returned the boy, a sudden flush covering his face as he spoke.

"You have come alone!—a little fellow like you—and on foot! Why, what were your father and mother thinking of, to let you take such a journey alone?"

"I have no mother, and my father does not care what I do," answered the child.

He spoke with calmness, but a certain trembling of the lip, a certain shadow in the eye, betrayed the emotion which he suppressed.

"No mother!—that's sad," returned the farmer's wife, as her keen gaze wandered from the dusky curls, and the pale, weary, unchildish face, to the little tired feet cased in worn shoes. "No mother!—that's sorrowful; and we have had a little quarrel with father, and we have run away—is that it?"

"No, that is a wrong guess, but I have run away—I don't deny that," said the child, lifting his eyes, and looking the good woman in the face bravely.

"Mercy alive!" she exclaimed. "Now what have you run away for? You are a little gentleman. You are no poor parish apprentice running from a hard master."

"No, I will never be an apprentice," he replied; "and I would rather not answer any more questions, thank you. Will you please tell me the way to Castle Crehylls?"

"Upon my word, my little man, any one would think you were a little lord to hear your way of talking," responded the good dame. "I only ask questions for your own good, my lad. I don't want you to get into trouble. If I was you I would go home again."

"I have no home," he replied. "I always stay at school in the holidays. Oh, please tell me the way to Crehylls."

Mrs. Chagwynne was too full of curiosity and perplexity to answer this question in a direct manner; moreover, the child's air and bearing puzzled her, and she had some vague idea in her mind that she ought to seize him and deliver him into the hands of the sleepy village constable, at this moment reposing on the settle at the Crehylls Arms.

"Now look here, my boy, I don't like to have anything to do with run-aways, and that's the truth," observed Mrs. Chagwynne; "so I don't think I shall show you the road to Crehylls, unless you tell me who you are, and what you are going there for."

"My name is Alfred Singleton, and I am going to see Lady Crehylls," said the boy, proudly.

"Lady Crehylls!" exclaimed Mrs. Chagwynne. "Well I never! I am sure I didn't mean to be rude, young gentleman. Are you related to the family? You've got a Crehylls' look on your face."

The boy made no answer, and the dame continued,—"Well, I expect you are akin to 'em in some way or other; so, if you like, I'll give you a lift on my horse. I go by Crehylls on my way home."

This proposition seemed to please the little traveller exceedingly well, and in a moment he was safely seated behind the stout Mrs. Chagwynne, who put her horse into a jog trot, at which pace he continued for three miles. By this time they had reached the brow of a steep hill, and here, in rather a breathless state, she drew rein.

"There's Castle Crehylls," she said, pointing into the deeply wooded valley below, where, amid the trees, there peeped the turrets of an ancient mansion. "The place is fine and ould, sure 'nough. Some folks says it's haunted, and some says it's whisht, and so it may be now, but in the former lord's time-—him that's dead, you know—I've see'd it gay as a feer (fair)."

With eager eyes the boy pressed forward, and looked down upon the old house.

"It is very beautiful," he said, in a whisper. "I have dreamed of it often."

"Then this isn't the first time you've seen Castle Crehylls?" observed keen Mrs. Chag-wynne; "and yet I don't mind my lady ever having little visitors like you. They say she can't abide the sight of children; and no wonder," she added, to herself. "Well, I suppose you were here in the old time, when my lord was alive. And yet, no—you are too young. How ould ar'ee, my dear?"

"I am nine years old," replied little Alfred Singleton; "and I was never at Crehylls before, that I know of."

It was evident that he fell in Mrs. Chag-wynne's estimation from this fact, for she made no reply as she guided the horse slowly down the steep descent. In the same silence she jogged along through the valley for half-a-mile, till the park gates rose before them, each pillar supporting in carved stone the Crehylls' crest, a mailed arm and hand grasping a dragon.

"What does that mean?" said Alfred Single-ton, pointing to the stone hand.

"Well, the story goes hereabouts," said Mrs. Chagwynne, "that in the ould times there was a fiery dragon in the land, and nothing would content him except the bones of little children. He devoured all he could find far and near, till at last the brave Baron Crehylls, who was one of King Arthur's knights, attacked him, and crushed him with his hands, thus saving the lives of all the little prisoners, who stood around trembling with fear. For this brave deed, a fairy said the house of Crehylls should never want an heir; and ever since that, you see, they've put the dragon over their gates, and on their carriages and seals."

"I suppose there were dragons once," said the child, in a dreamy tone. "But it doesn't sound like a true story."

"It isn't true in one thing," returned Mrs. Chagwynne; "for there is no heir now to the house of Crehylls, and there never will be. So when my lord dies—and he is but a wisht body—the title will go too, and there'll be only a little maid to take the money and the lands. But la! my dear, what do you care about these things? I'm very foolish to talk of them."

"But I care very much, ma'am," returned her young companion, while a sudden colour flashed over his face. "Please tell me why all the lands go to a little girl?"

"Because Lord Crehylls has got no boy," she replied; "he had three, but they all died very young—that's why my lady can't bear the sight of children, they say—and now his only child is a girl, whom he dotes on. Well, here we are at the gate! Jump down and open it, my son. Now shall I stop and ax for the housekeeper for 'ee, or will 'ee go in by yourself, my dear?"

"But you have brought me in the back way," said the child, recoiling.

"You don't think that such as you and I could be impertinent enough to come in by the great gates?" cried Mrs. Chagwynne. "There, my son, go on, and ax for the housekeeper."

"But I don't want her. I want Lady Crehylls," persisted the child.

Somewhat frightened at bringing this unknown waif to Crehylls, Mrs. Chagwynne looked around the spacious yard with a bewildered air, her face, however, clearing as she caught sight of a red head emerging from an out-house.

"Dick! here, Dick!" she cried. "Here's a little master wants my lady, and he wont see nobody but her."

Dick regarded the little wanderer curiously, and then grinned from ear to ear.—"My lady isn't in," said he, "and my lord is out."

"If you please, then, I'll wait," said the child, in the patient voice that seemed peculiar to him.

"Don't make game of the boy, Dick," expostulated Mrs. Chagwynne. "Can't you manage for him to have speech with my lady?"

"Well, if you'll get off your hoss and hinter-duce him, p'raps I may," retorted Dick.

This proposition evidently frightened Mrs. Chagwynne, for she gathered up the reins hastily.

"Oh, I don't know nothing about him," she said, twisting the horse's head round with a jerk. "I picked 'im up in the road because he was tired, that's all. And I reckon I must ride home fast; it's getting late."

Upon this Mrs. Chagwynne departed, but not, however, without a wistful look at the forlorn little figure in the courtyard, who felt, as she rode away, that his only friend was gone. And there he stood, quiet, patient, and enduring, while Dick cleaned innumerable knives with the air of taking his pleasure.

"Well, there's the last of 'em," said he, at length, depositing the last batch in a tray.

"And, now you have finished, will you please take me to Lady Crehylls?" asked the patient watcher.

Highly amused at the request, Dick responded, with mock civility, "Where's your little lord-ship's card? I couldn't announce you without your card."

"You are laughing at me," returned the boy; "and oh, I want to see Lady Crehylls so much!"

He could scarcely keep back the tears now,

but, suppressing them with an effort, he clasped his small hands together, and still stood in pa-tient hopefulness before his tormentor.

" You're a very particler friend of my lady's, I s'pose," said Dick, whistling softly to himself; " but where's the coach and four you comed in the last time you were here? We are a impercut lot at Crehylls; we aint got no respect for folks standin' in their own shoes; they must alwis have a hoss under 'em, or a carridge; then, bless you! the door flies open like winking. Go back and fetch your coach-and-four, and don't, 'pon no account, forget your card."

With this parting advice, amicably bestowed, Dick shambled off with his tray of knives.

Grooms and stable-boys going to and fro, or loitering in the yard, had taken small notice of the dialogue between Dick and the little wistful, shabby figure standing by him; but now, when the child addressed them in a piteous voice, asking to be taken to Lady Crehylls, they stopped to stare and laugh.

" Did the parson send you?" said one.

" No, I came of my own accord," replied the boy, looking from one to the other with brave eyes and a pale face.

The men shrugged their shoulders at this reply, and most of them turned away to their work.

" It isn't no good loitering about here," ob-served a groom. " My lady can't abide beggars."

"I am no beggar!" cried the child, indignantly. But the cruel word had struck the chord, whose tension was pulling at his heart, and covering his white, wistful face with both his hands, he burst into tears. Yet considering his tender years, and the bitterness of his thoughts, he recovered himself quickly, and, like some little wan shadow, he flitted away in such patient silence, that they scarce knew when he was gone.

The long summer evening faded with all its purple glories into the grey dimness of a June night, and the soft moon and stars looked down upon the pale face of little Alfred Singleton, slumbering by the way-side, in the great sombre shadow of Castle Crehylls.

CHAPTER XVIII

THE sunshine lay glittering on southern slopes, mingled with sharp shadows, clear as cut steel, while the woods, unshaken by a breath of wind, stood as motionless as though a fairy, with a sudden wand, had struck them into an enchanted sleep. Unclouded by a fleecy speck, the sky, deep blue, hung high above the seething landscape, and hazily blending with its sapphire dome, loomed the great hills purplish and mystic. Nearer to the eye rose tall single trees, drooping with heat, still as sentinels, every limb and leaf sharply defined against the quiet air, their shadows lying crisp upon the shining green. Beneath these the fainting cattle stretched themselves uneasily, with a weary look of pain in their patient eyes. And down in the dells, panting sheep sought the small shelter that the shade of a hedge could give, as like a ribbon long drawn out, it rested on the sward—a narrow strip of grey. Silently the tired mowers plied their scythes, with thirst upon their lips, and in the lanes, where drooping roses

shed their leaves upon the dust, heavily-laden
waggons went creaking home, slowly shaking on
the sultry air the scent of fragrant hay. The
primroses were dead, and the violets slept, but
upon every hedge the honeysuckle clustered,
a very wilderness of sweets, and the columbine
hung its purple crown, amid peeping periwinkle
and trailing morning-glories. Such a wealth of
perfume, such a wealth of colour, all spread
silently beneath the summer sun, as in the
fierceness of his strength he mounted the ambient
sky.

Oh the long, long day—how slowly it rose to
the zenith, how slowly it sank to the wane!
And as the languid hours crept wearily on, a
child watched the shadows lengthen, with wistful
eyes fixed upon Crehylls. With a patient perseverance characteristic of his nature, he sat
over against the mansion, waiting, hoping, longing, wearying for the great doors to open,
dreaming he should see issue forth, coming
towards him with kindly smile, the graceful
lady who had pitied him in the churchyard
of Penkivel.

What a strange picture the little forlorn
figure made, seated on that secluded hillock in
the park, watching with big tearful eyes the
glaring castle, seeing it change from glistening
white to grey, seeing here and there a sign of
dainty life about its stately shadow; but

never, never seeing the presence for which he longed.

" Will she never come?" he said; and tears, long repressed, fell down fast on the pale, pinched cheeks of the little wanderer.   Then he brushed them away and watched again, renewing the fainting hope in his childish heart with whispered words of comfort, and thoughts of ancient stories of little children, like himself, who had been brave and patient, and through constancy had won to fortune.   He thought of Whittington sitting on the stone by the wayside hungry and faint, wondering where he should lay his head.

" But I'll never turn back like Whittington," he said; and forthwith his large wistful eyes, gathering brightness from the resolve within him, glanced upwards to the sky, smiling with hope and prayer.

Once or twice he opened the tiny bundle, which he kept so carefully by his side, and took thence a piece of bread, which some kind heart had given him the day before, as his small feet trailed wearily on the dusty way.   This was all the food he had; but he drank often of the brook that ran close by, babbling to him as it went, such strange and beautiful dreams of the unknown world, that jaded men and heartless women, could they have read them, as they rose before those pure fresh eyes, would have turned away their heads in shame, and wept in bitterness.

The day was long, but perhaps to him the sun's strength was tempered, and the sultry hours passed softly over the small bowed head that in such gentle patience watched their flight.

But ah! it was hard to see the sun go down, and yet catch no glimpse of the kind face, for which he had waited, with such wondrous steadfastness, through the long, long summer day. So as the shadows grew thick about him, creeping darkly to his feet like dim ghosts of dead Crehylls, his spirits sank, his grief, his loneliness, his terrors came crowding on his heart at once, and with sobs and tears he fell on his knees to pray. In his childish anguish the words dropped from his lips aloud—" Lord have mercy on me! I am only a little child. I have waited and trusted all the day. Bring me to the dear, kind lady—let me see her face. Give me food and shelter. I am afraid of this loneliness. I am afraid to sleep upon the ground again. Help me, dear Lord! help a little child, who has no home."

As his simple prayer ceased, a slight sound made him lift his head from his hands, and there, standing beneath the bank, he saw a tiny creature dressed in white, with face like an angel's, regarding him with grave surprise and tearful sympathy.

" Are you praying to see mamma?" she said. " Come with me, and I will lead you to her."

She climbed the steep bank as she spoke, and held out her hand to him. Ashamed of his tears, he turned his face from her shyly, not daring to take the little extended hand ; but she seized his with gentle force, and bending over him, for he was still kneeling, she kissed him suddenly and wiped his tears away with her handkerchief.

"Don't cry any more, poor boy," she said, pitifully. "Come to mamma now ; she is on the seat there beneath the May-tree."

Hand in hand they descended the bank together, the boy, who with such steady purpose, such wondrous patience, had waited throughout the day, depressed now and silent, the girl full of prattle and of questions. Obliged to rally to reply to them, he became unconsciously more self-possessed, more erect in mien, and as he spoke of his wrongs, the cruelties of the coward Whalley, and his own resolve to go out into the world alone, his eyes flashed, and there came into his pale cheeks a tinge of colour. Then the girl grew silent, looking on him with a gaze full of innocence and wonder.

It was thus the children presented themselves before a lady, propped with cushions, reclining on a seat placed beneath a group of hawthorns, whose dying blossoms sprinkled her as she lay.

"Mamma," said the child, gently.

The lady raised her head languidly from the

cushion, and the little Alfred saw a face wan as a shadow, pale with the suffering of long sickness; but it was not the face that had bent over him lovingly in the churchyard of Penkivel. Struck with chill dismay and disappointment, he grasped his little companion's hand in a tighter clasp, and stood silent and trembling.

The lady gazed upon the two children, with a strange shadow of perplexity deepening in her eyes. She saw upon their young faces a mutual likeness that startled her—a likeness not to be denied or mistaken. There is a something mysterious, which marks the faces and bearing of every family, enabling us to recognise in a moment those who are of the same blood. In the lineage of the Crehylls this seal of race and of resemblance lay upon the forehead and brows, giving to the face of each scion of the family what the country people called the "Crehylls-look." It was an earnest look—a contraction of the brow, denoting patience and perseverance. Of late years, enervated perhaps by wealth, this patience in the race had degenerated into weakness, and their ancient name, Crehylls—crushed, —adopted by the ancestor who slew the dragon, seemed more adapted to express their sufferings than their prowess. Now, this steadfast Crehylls look upon the children's faces, as they stood with brows the counterpart each of each, brought a flush of wonder to the invalid's pale cheeks.

"This is mamma," said the little girl, dragging Alfred forward : "this is Lady Crehylls."

"No," returned the boy, dropping her hand with a patient sigh, "that is not Lady Crehylls —that is not the lady I want to see."

"Who is your companion, Lydia ?" said Lady Crehylls, a little sternly.

The tone of her mother's voice struck the little creature painfully ; she gave one wistful look on the wan, weary figure, whose hand had just unclasped hers, and then rushing impetuously forward, she clasped her arms round the neck of the sick lady.

"Mamma," she whispered very low, " I heard him praying. He asked God to send him to Lady Crehylls ; and he said he was lonely and afraid—afraid to lie on the ground again, mamma. He said, too, that he had no home, and he asked God to pity him. Dear mamma, you have told me that wicked children never pray ; so I thought he was good, and I might bring him to you."

The lady listened to her little daughter quietly, except for a slight trembling of the lip, and then she kissed her.

"Doubtless you have done right, Lydia," she said ; "but let us hear what the little boy has to say for himself."

"Oh, mamma," interrupted Lydia, in an earnest whisper, "don't let him know I have told you what I heard. It would be so cruel.

And he says he has run away from a wicked schoolmaster."

Raising herself on her fragile arm, Lady Crehylls beckoned Alfred Singleton to draw nearer.

"What is your name?" she said, "and why do you wish to see me? Is it true you have run away?"

"Yes; I have walked from Exeter," he answered. "It is a fortnight ago since I got out of the window in the early morning, and ran away. I hid in the woods till nightfall, then I walked as far as I could and hid again. It was very lonely in the woods. I was afraid, and cried sometimes; but I never thought of stopping or of going back."

"So you have run away from school?" said Lady Crehylls, gravely.

For a moment the boy hung his head abashed, then he raised his eyes to hers and clasped his hands nervously.

"If you knew all, you would not be angry," he said. "Two of the boys have agreed to kill themselves if their fathers send them back next half; and last month I saw a little boy die at school. He was smaller than me, and Mr. Whalley beat him till he fell down. Then they carried him to bed, and in the night I stole into his room, and put my arm about his neck. 'Is that you, Alf?' he said. 'Kiss me, dear.' And when I kissed him his face was cold. 'Don't stay here to die like me, Alf,' he whispered. 'Run away, else you'll be killed too.'"

"And did the poor child die?" asked Lady Crehylls, in a tone of horror.

"He was quite cold when I stole away from his bedside," answered the little Alfred, simply. "He had no father and mother, and his uncle is in India. No one said anything when he was buried."

"It appears to me you did quite right to escape from such a master," returned Lady Crehylls, glancing wistfully on her own child. "But, my dear, why did you not go home?"

"I have no home," said the boy, clasping and unclasping his thin, small fingers as he spoke. "My mother is dead, and I don't know where my father lives. Mr. Whalley always sent my letters to him. He does not care for me, I think."

The dreary, quiet tone in which he spoke had a pathos in it past description. It pierced the heart of Lady Crehylls with a deep pang, filled as it was with forebodings of the coming orphanage of her own child.

"Oh, your father loves you, my dear," she said, wistfully. "You must not think otherwise. Tell me why you came to Crehylls."

"I thought to see the lady," returned Alfred Singleton; "she told me to come to her, if I needed a friend. Here is her letter."

He took it from between the leaves of a book
in the little bundle he carried, and handed it
to Lady Crehylls. There she read these few
words :—

" DEAR CHILD,—Remember I am called Lady
Crehylls, and should you need a friend, come to
me without fear, and I will help you. Keep
this letter, lest you should forget my name, and
bear this firmly in mind, that I am your friend,
"AGATHA CREHYLLS."

" This letter is from the Dowager Lady
Crehylls, my sister-in-law," said the sick lady.
" You should have gone to Penkivel, my dear;
she lives there !"

"I asked all the people I met where Lady
Crehylls lived," answered Alfred; " and they
said at Castle Crehylls. Please, how far is it to
Penkivel? Can I get there to-night if I walk
fast ?"

The patient bearing of the boy, as shouldering
his bundle again he stood prepared to start forth
once more on a weary journey, struck Lady
Crehylls with sorrowful admiration. All her
boys were dead. If her favourite, if Lawrence
had lived, he, too, would have had an undaunted
spirit like this little stranger. Ah! how proud
she would have felt at his courage ! With
wistful eyes she looked upon Alfred Singleton's

flushing face, and laid her hand kindly on his arm.

"You cannot walk to Penkivel, my boy," said she. "You shall stay here to-night, and to-morrow we will send you to my sister's in a carriage. Penkivel is more than thirty miles away. Now, my love," she continued, turning to her little girl, "call the servants to help me in. I am tired, and it grows cold."

"May I go with her?" asked Alfred, eagerly.

Lady Crehylls smiled and nodded. So the children went away hand in hand again, but in a moment Lydia ran back.

"Mamma," she whispered, "if the little boy is a friend of Aunt Agatha's, may he not be my friend too? Please don't send him away so soon as to-morrow. I am so lonely here. I have no one to play with, you know, but you."

The dying lady could scarcely repress her tears. Lonely!—was her child lonely now? Oh what was this loneliness to that greater pain drawing nearer and nearer day by day!

"Aunt Agatha's friend," she repeated, thoughtfully. "Yes, darling, her friends may always be your friends too. The little boy may stay longer than to-morrow if he likes."

"Oh, I know he'll like to stay!" cried Lydia. "You dear, good mamma, how kind you are!" and kissing her, she ran off eagerly to rejoin her little companion.

"The boy is a gentleman's son evidently," observed Lady Crehylls to herself. "I cannot have done wrong. Perhaps he is some poor clergyman's child. Agatha is always kind to orphans. Doubtless she knew his father and his family, or she would not have written to the child."

CHAPTER XIX

T was the first night of a new opera, and as the last song of the finale quivered in the ear, a hundred " Bravos !" rent the air, and on the stage, the centre figure of a picturesque group, stood Madame Silvia, curtseying and smiling, as she received the plaudits of the audience. Her face was flushed with triumph, and over her bending figure there rested a grace that charmed every eye. Suddenly, from a large box near the stage, there fell a magnificent bouquet at the singer's feet; and as she stooped and gathered it up, she glanced at the donor, a small, spare man, with a star upon his breast. A glow of pleasure covered his face as her eyes met his, and he smiled and bowed hurriedly. But there was no answering smile on Madame Silvia's lips as she curtseyed to him deeply ; and as the green curtain fell, she dropped the flowers scornfully, and moved away, letting them lie unregarded on the boards. Then a gentleman, who from the side-scenes had witnessed the finale, and this little interlude of the flowers,.

came hastily forward, and offered the prima donna his arm.

"Madeline," he said, in a low voice, "I saw the duke annoy you again to-night. Why will you continue to expose yourself to such insults? Have you not had enough yet of this meretricious triumph, this noise and show?"

"Noise and show!" she repeated. "I sing for my bread, not for triumphs." And looking down upon the nosegay of rare flowers, she thrust it aside with her foot, as she spoke. "And if I have to accept such things as this, as the consequences of my position, would it not be a folly in me to fret at them?"

During this short dialogue, the clamour and the cries of "encore" had become so vociferous that, yielding to the demand of the audience, a signal was given for the curtain to rise again. Then the actors hastily grouped themselves, the gentleman on whose arm Madame Silvia leaned, sprang aside, while she gathered up the fallen flowers, and as the curtain rose, and she faced the audience, she put them to her smiling lips. A momentary burst of applause, then a lull, and in that silence the clear, powerful voice of Madame Silvia rose in glorious melody, pouring forth the solo in the finale. The chorus answered, swelled, and died away, and once more the heroine fell in the arms of her lover, pouring forth her dying song in "linked sweetness long drawn out;"

then again the curtain descended, and the satisfied audience slowly melted away, But on the stage the crowd increased each moment, actors, manager, and visitors, all pressing round Madame Silvia to congratulate her on her success. She seemed to have a word and a smile for every one, yet she none the less made her way steadily towards her dressing-room, the door of which was closed against the crowd. In a few minutes she emerged, clothed in sober grey, with a large cloak wrapped about her, and then the gentleman on whose arm she had leaned before, came forward and offered it again. But at the same instant a small thin voice accosted her.

"Madame Silvia surpassed herself to-night," said the voice. "Her singing and acting were both superb."

Her hand dropped from the arm it had scarcely touched, and with lips slightly paling, she turned and greeted the new comer.

"I am glad you think so, duke," she replied. "I am proud I have pleased so fastidious a critic."

"You always please me," returned the duke, lowering his voice to a whisper. "But where are your flowers?" he continued aloud. "I thought Madame Silvia had deigned to accept my poor gift."

"My flowers!" said the lady, hurriedly. "Is it possible I have forgotten my flowers? I must have left them in my room. I'll go and fetch them."

But twenty obsequious messengers were there to save her the trouble, and in a moment the bouquet was placed in her hand.

"I hope the flowers are not soiled," said the gentleman who brought them. "I found them on the floor; they had fallen from the table, I suppose."

"Duke, will you permit us to say good-night?" observed the gentleman by Madame Silvia's side. "I fear my horses will take cold."

"Sir, I have not the slightest wish to detain you," said the duke. "Pray attend at once to the health of your horses. Mine can wait as long as Madame Silvia pleases."

He said this gaily, in that tone of merriment which takes away half the offence; but it did not prevent an angry reply from rising to the other's lips.

"I believe Madame Silvia will care very little how long or how short a time your horses wait, duke, since she does me the honour to return home in my carriage."

"Maurice, are you mad?" whispered Madame Silvia, earnestly. "I can't offend this man."

In an instant she had turned to the duke, and accosted him with a flattering smile, and a certain bewitching coquetry in her manner, indescribable in words. Maurice watched her

moodily, but without making any effort to inter-
rupt a conversation from which the crowd gently
drew apart, as though they regarded it as a *tête-à-
tête*.

"Do not flatter me," said the duke. "You
are cold as ice, and as white and smooth.
But what does that matter? I love you all the
same."

These words were spoken in Italian; and as he
uttered them, a faint flush rose in Madame
Silvia's ivory face.

"The time will come," she said, and her lip
shook, "when men will wonder, why an insult to
one of my profession was so easy and so safe."

"Do you suppose, that it is because I see you
here that I venture to tell you, that your heart
is cold as ice?" asked the duke. "No, it is
because I know Madame Silvia as well as I
knew Madeline Sylvester. Look in the flowers
before you fling them away again; you will find
something there, that you would be sorry for a
servant to read."

"I will take care of your flowers," said
Madame Silvia, hiding her fear and hatred in a
smooth voice. "Good night, duke. Maurice, I
am ready."

The gentleman, whom she thus accosted, conducted her silently to the carriage awaiting them,
and placed her within it, then he lifted his hat,
and gave her a cold good night.

"What folly!" she cried, with a silvery laugh. "Do you suppose I will take your carriage, and let you walk home? No, indeed! Call a coach for me, if you please," she said, turning to the servant. "I will not return home in Mr. Pellew's carriage."

On hearing this Maurice Pellew turned, and laid his hand for one wavering moment on the door of the chariot, then he sprung up the steps, and took his seat by the side of the woman who still held him captive.

"Maurice, you are unreasonable to be angry," she said, after an instant's silence. "Would I be civil to that detestable man, unless circumstances compelled me?"

"I can see no circumstances," began Maurice.

"You are mistaken," she interposed. "Two men in London have recognised, in Madame Silvia, that unhappy Madeline Sylvester whom Lady Crehylls slandered. These two are yourself and this Russian with a French name, the Duke de Briancourt."

"And what then?" asked Maurice.

"And then, what seems so slight a thing to you might be a great misfortune to me. Hundreds, perhaps thousands, unable to account otherwise for the exile of Lord Crehylls, still believe the cruel, wicked slander, circulated by his wife. How eagerly the world would revive the lie, if it knew that I was Madeline Sylvester! Hands that applauded me yesterday would be ready to stone me to-morrow. My innocence would have no more effect on the crowd, than it had formerly on you. And I should leave my art, which I love so much, in contempt and anger——"

"As you left me," interrupted Maurice.

Madeline's eye flashed on him a strange look, but she permitted the reproach to remain unanswered.

"The love of my art," she continued, "is the last faithful, forlorn love left me. Let me keep it if I can. It is for this I am civil to the Duke de Briancourt. He can tell the world who I am; he can drive me into solitude, where I should soon die."

"Is this all your reason?" asked Maurice, with the old jealous ring in his voice.

"No, not all," she replied. "I confess I am civil to this man from fear. I have the same unaccountable terror of him, which I had when almost a child at Florence—which I had when a girl; I met him again in London, and fled to the Singletons from his cruel pursuit of me."

"Ah, Madeline, why not have appealed to me for help?" said Maurice.

"How easily you shift the blame of that time from yourself to me," she returned, a little scornfully. "How could I appeal to you for help?— you who had insulted and forsaken me—you who, through your mother, pursued me with a renewed and vindictive insult?"

"Madeline, you know now I was innocent of that cruel wrong to me and yourself," said Maurice.

"I know it; but what then? It does not undo the past—it does not give me back my life," she replied, bitterly.

"If you had only had patience, Madeline," continued Maurice, "all would have been well. Explanation and forgiveness must have come in time."

"How could I have patience?" she said. "I was writhing beneath a cruel slander. I was terrified by one lover, and forsaken by the other. And I, who had accepted gall from all the world, found I could not take the cup from your hands. I rushed impulsively into a hasty marriage, wronging a good man, and heaping on my own heart a heavy load of remorse and sorrow. No! why do I say I did it? Agatha Crehylls' was the hand which brought the evil upon you, upon me, and upon one, whose soul was the noblest and gentlest in the world. And he died striving to save her child," she added, with an indescribable · accent of bitterness, "died just when I thought to be happier——"

Tears sprang to her eyes, and she stopped suddenly. Maurice listened to her words with a sinking heart. He felt that her love for him had died away, or she could not praise another man in his hearing; she could not regret another love in his presence. The explanation they had mutually given of the past had made them friends, nothing more.

When Maurice Pellew would have spoken of love, when he looked wistfully into Madeline's face, seeking there some ray of hope, some lingering gleam of the old tenderness, he found only an icy calm, or a reserve he could not penetrate. He had thought at first it would be easy to assume his old sway, but time had taught him otherwise; and now, though three months had passed since he and Madeline had met again, the silent barrier between them stood firm as ever.

" Do you regret the past so much?" he said, in a vexed tone.

" It is not regret I feel, it is remorse," she answered, in a hard voice.

" Remorse ! " he exclaimed. " I thought that might be mine, but not yours. What do you repent, Madeline ?"

" I repent a deed of hasty impulsive generosity," she replied, gloomily ; " when I should only have considered justice, I gave way to romance, not counting the cost. From this has sprung all my sorrows and my sins. I have spared others, but they never spared me."

This was the first time she had referred to the primary cause of their quarrel, and Maurice answered her eagerly.

" You allude to the man whom you supposed guilty of the death of Carbis ?" he said. " Madeline, I guessed long ago that Lord Crehylls was this man. He was innocent, I am certain. Let me speak earnestly with you on this matter on some future day, and be frank with me, I entreat you. You say that you repent of your romance; then now let us do sober justice and repair the past if possible."

" Justice ! " she echoed—" it is too late for that : it degenerates into revenge now. And—and, Maurice, do you know that sometimes I am hateful to myself ? If it were not for my life upon the stage I should go mad ! "

She spoke vehemently, and the sudden stopping of the carriage made her voice sound strangely wild.

" Are we arrived already ?" she said, relapsing swiftly into languor. " I will not ask you in, Maurice, it is so late; but I do not act to-morrow evening, so you can dine with me, if agreeable to you."

" You may be sure of seeing me," returned Maurice, grasping her hand eagerly.

She was alighting from the carriage now, but with her foot on the last step she stood an instant, her hand still in his.

" Congratulate me on my courage," she said. " Do you know my little ward is lost ? And yet, you see, I have not shed a tear, or broken down in the part I had to sing."

" Lost ! " exclaimed Maurice.

" Yes, he has run away from school," she replied, " and perhaps perished by the road-side ; he may be lying now dead or dying, unnamed and unknown, in some poor workhouse."

" Do not torment yourself with so dreadful a picture," said Mr. Pellew. " The child is safe doubtless."

" Can it matter what becomes of him ?" she asked. " Does the world usually care whether the child of a villain dies in a ditch or no ?"

The lamplight fell full upon her face, as, with these bitter words upon her lips, she smiled and passed within the house.

" I forgot the boy is Rathline's," said Maurice to himself. But his gaze was still fixed and wondering, and when the closed door had hidden Madeline from his sight, his eyes seemed still to see the vision of that graceful figure and scornful face.

" Where to, sir ?" said the servant, breaking in upon his thoughts.

" Home," he answered, drearily.

As the carriage wended its way through the darkening streets, Maurice Pellew mused and wondered at the woman he had left. When it set him down, his thoughts were busy with the same theme, and in his lonely room, he still strove, like a man working out a problem, to understand and reconcile in his mind the incongruous phases of her strange character. But in all his wild thoughts of her, not one so wild as the truth presented itself to his imagination. No, he never dreamed of her as kneeling before her desk reading those early letters, which he wrote to her in the first happiness of their betrothal; he never pictured her with tears streaming down her cheeks, as with haggard eyes she pored over these records of the love, she dared not now accept.

16—2

CHAPTER XX.

HY didn't he say he knowed Lady Crehylls, of Penkivel?" asked the astounded Dick of his fellow-servants. "Who would think a gen'leman's son would come trapesing here a-foot like a beggar?"

"When a boy runs away from school," returned an indignant footman, "he ain't usual got pocket money enough to buy a coach-and-four. You should have called me, when the young gentleman asked for Lady Crehylls. I should have known better than to answer him like a gawking idiot."

"Well, never mind," said a housemaid, who pitied the abashed Dick, "the child is doing well now,—he wont die this time. I'm sure I never see my lady more anxious for one of her own than she's been for him; and as to Miss Lydia, she nearly cried her heart out when he lay ill. I wonder who the boy is? My lord and my lady haven't said nothing about him; but of course he's related to the family."

"Any one can see that," observed another, mysteriously.

This talk took place three days after the arrival of the little Alfred Singleton at Castle Crehylls—three days during which he had struggled with the fever, and exhaustion of fatigue and famine. It seemed very strange to the little sufferer to be nursed gently,—stranger still to find kind eyes watching him when he awoke from his uneasy slumber, or tossed restless on his bed. But now, on this third day, he was able to get up; and ensconced in a great arm-chair, so big that he seemed lost in it, he sat near a sunny window, very demure and thoughtful, with his small white face bearing more legibly on his brow that strange seal of steadfast patience. But this was suddenly brightened by a smile, as a soft step drew near him, and a little hand timidly touched his.

"Are you better?" said Lydia. "Mamma has sent you these strawberries; and I have brought you my new picture-book to look at."

"I am much better, thank you," replied Alfred. "I think I shall be able to go to Penkivel to-morrow."

"Mamma wont let you go to-morrow," returned Lydia, as a shadow fell over her rosy face. "She has promised that I shall show you my new swing in the elm avenue, and the nest of little goldfinches, and my pony."

Lydia's possessions and Lydia's happy looks

seemed ever a new source of wonder to the child, whose few years were crowded with painful memories.

"Have you a pony?" he said, eagerly; "a pony all your own?"

"Yes, and I've a long habit, and a pretty whip with a gold handle, that mamma gave me," replied Lydia.

"Then your mamma loves you?" said Alfred, looking in her face earnestly.

That her mother's love should be a matter of wonder, or of question, seemed strange indeed to Lydia, and revolving this new idea in her childish mind, there crept into it a shadow of the forlornness of the little wistful questioner, whose eyes were fixed on hers. She gazed into his face in a grave, sad way, as though marking how white and wasted it was, and how it bore in its youthful lines an unnatural thought-fulness, and look of unchildish care. Perhaps she saw all this but dimly, having scarcely sense to shape it into thought, but she felt it as the blind feel colours; and the loneliness, the sorrow, the anguish of the poor, forlorn, unloved boy fell like a shadow upon her spirit.

"I am so sorry," she said, softly, as her arm stole about his neck; "I wish you had a mamma that loved you; but, if you stay here, you may have my mamma to be your mamma, too, and you can be my little brother, if you like. You know my real brothers are dead. I'll show you their pictures when you are better."

In his superior age and wisdom the little Alfred smiled at her proposition, and, boy like, he took her caresses quietly, not giving back one.

" I can't be your brother," he said. "Your papa wont let me. I am only a poor boy; I shall have to work very hard when I am a man, while you will be a rich lady, with this great castle all your own."

" But if you were my brother, I could give half to you," said Lydia; " and then you would not be poor. Say, will you have it?" she asked, pressing her round, rosy cheek against his wan face.

" When you are bigger, you wont ask me," said Alfred; " you wont care to have a brother like me then."

" Yes, I shall," returned Lydia, sturdily. " I have heard mamma say she wished I had a brother, and I have seen her cry often, when she looked at me playing by myself. I know she'll let me have you for a brother. Shall I go and ask her?"

" No, not yet," said Alfred, holding her tightly in the span of his small arm; " I'm afraid she'll keep you with her then, and I want you to stay with me, and show me these pictures. I shall like you for a sister very much. I can take you for my sister, you know, without asking any one."

This arrangement contenting Lydia completely, Alfred made room for her on his big chair, and with the book of engravings on their laps they sat with clasped hands, and small intent faces, turning over the pictures gravely.

It was thus the easy, indolent Lord Crehylls found them, and looking at them in his absent way, he thought they made a pretty picture— no, it was a striking picture—because of the contrast between Lydia's rosy happiness and the little stranger's wan look of sorrow. Then there came into his dreamy mind some hazy thought of danger to his child, and he called suddenly, "Lydia!"

Sauntering into the room with his soft step, with one book in his hand and another in his pocket, the children had not heard him; but now, startled, both looked up, and Alfred Single-ton, flushing painfully, strove to rise, but being weak and trembling, fell back in the chair again, while Lydia, with both arms round him, rebuked him gravely for the effort.

"Lydia," said Lord Crehylls, "little Lanyon hasn't got anything catching, has he?—fever, or anything of that sort."

"Oh no, papa," said Lydia; "he is only tired; there's nothing the matter with him at all but that."

"Very well, my dear. No, I daresay not. Of course your mamma would not have let you play with him if——"

But here Lord Crehylls' eye fell upon his open book, and he became absorbed immediately in its pages.

"If you please," said the little Alfred.

But Lord Crehylls made him no answer. Then he waited patiently till the reader moved his eyes for a single instant from the book as he turned a page.

"If you please," began the quiet voice again.

"Eh!—what! Is it you, little Lanyon, speaking?" asked Lord Crehylls.

"If you please, sir—my lord—I wanted to say, that my name is not Lanyon," replied the child.

"Not Lanyon!" said Lord Crehylls. "Dear me! I thought you were related to my brother's widow. I thought you brought a letter from Agatha. Not Lanyon! Here, Caroline," cried the helpless man, looking around on the four walls for his wife. "So your mamma isn't here," he said, bewildered. "Lydia, where is your mother?"

"Mamma is not so well to-day," replied Lydia. "She is lying down in her room, papa."

"Not so well? Poor thing! I'll go to her." So saying, Lord Crehylls fell into the nearest chair, and lost himself in his book again. But the little Alfred Singleton was too brave, and too honest to remain tranquil under the idea, that he was supposed to be a relative of the beautiful lady, whom he had seen in the churchyard of Penkivel. So, in spite of Lydia's small restraining arms, he got down feebly from the big chair and crept, with trembling steps, to the reader's side. Here his small shadow fell quiveringly on the book, and Lord Crehylls looked up surprised.

"Eh! what! little Lanyon! You look very white; don't you think you would be better in bed, my dear?"

"I want to tell you," said Alfred, "that my name is Singleton, and I am not related to Lady Crehylls."

"Dear me!" returned the embarrassed nobleman, "I am sorry for that; but I suppose it does not matter much, does it? I understood we were to take care of you for a few days, till Agatha sent for you, and I assure you Lady Crehylls and I are very pleased to do anything to oblige her. So I hope, little Lanyon—Singleton, I mean—you have everything you want."

Here Lord Crehylls plunged all his sense into his book once more, and while Alfred for an instant felt afraid to speak, Lydia joined him, and stole her hand into his.

"Don't tell papa anything more," she whispered.

" But I must tell—I ought to tell," persisted Alfred aloud.

" Eh! what is it? what's the matter?" said Lord Crehylls.

" Oh, do please let me tell you all the truth," cried Alfred. " I've run away from school, that's the truth. And I mean to walk to Penkivel to see Lady Crehylls, but she does not know I am coming. And I cannot tell whether she will be as kind to me as you have been, for I have never seen her but once in all my life."

The earnestness in the small pale face, and the emphasis on " all my life,"—the little, fragile life, so few in years, so innocent, and yet so full of sorrow,—struck even the absent Lord Crehylls as something strange. He exerted himself so far as to close his book, and taking the trembling boy upon his knee, he began to question him; but ere he had received the answers, a frightened servant looked within the room, and with fingers held up and pale face, she beckoned to her master.

" My lord," she said, in a low, hurried voice, " there is a great change in my poor lady. Come and see her."

It was a change indeed; and soon throughout the castle, from roof to basement, there crept the chill whisper of coming death. Yet the lady lingered still a day or two, while hope clung with agonizing grasp upon her husband's heart, and the children, dimly conscious of the truth, played with hushed voices. On the last evening of her life she asked for them, and putting her hand upon their heads, she blessed them both. Some untold thought, some strange, prophetic instinct, was in her heart when she did this, and above all, when she gazed into their faces with a wistful, longing look of love.

"Do you see this strange likeness, Lawrence?" she said, faintly, to her husband. "I could not refuse help to a child coming to me, with that look upon his face. Ask Agatha who he is, and what you can do for him. Doubtless she knows more than he knows of himself, or she would not have written to the child. As I look upon his face I think——"

But her strength was gone, and Lord Crehylls was destined never to hear what her thought was. Agitated and overwhelmed with grief, he scarcely paused to wonder at her interest in the little waif that had strayed to Crehylls.

A few hours later in the night her spirit fled; and the two children, who had so strangely been brought together were left defenceless in the world.

CHAPTER XXI

N the west side of the park, about a mile from the castle, was a small garden, known as " My Lady's Garden." It was perfectly secluded, and hedged in from prying eyes on every side by a great wall of laurel. Throughout all England, there was said to be no such laurel hedge as this. Thick, green, and shining, and growing to a height of thirty feet or more, it encompassed the garden like a glossy rampart, shutting out the world. In this secluded place, two days after the death of Lady Crehylls, the children sat together. The nurse had thought that Miss Lydia ought not to be seen in the park, but in this quiet spot she might breathe the air unseen by the world, and forget her grief for the moment in the sunshine.

On the first day of her loss the child had wept in such terrible agony, that even in this short while her cheek had grown pale, and her rounded form had shrunk. Changed thus, there was a stranger, sadder likeness between her and the little Alfred Singleton : the kinship of sorrow was on their faces now.

The children sat on a grassy bank, Lydia with her lap full of flowers, which she arranged silently in a wreath, the little quivering lip and the quiet tears which fell slowly, telling whither her thoughts wandered; Alfred, on his knees beside her, cut the flowers the desired length, watching her the while in such awed curiosity and pity, that when he spoke his voice uttered itself in whispers.

"The wreath is for mamma," said Lydia; "papa told me to make it for her; she always loved flowers."

"I think heaven is full of flowers," answered Alfred. "Don't cry any more, Lydia. God wont send your mamma down from heaven, if you cry ever so bitterly. When I was little I used to cry a great deal; but I know better now."

"Why did you cry when you were little?" asked Lydia.

"I was so sorrowful," he answered. "I cried first to go home when I woke up, and found myself in a strange place. My own room had a marble floor and a high ceiling with angels on it. I used to dream about them often when I was little, and fancy they came down and kissed me; but the room I was in now, after I fell into the sea, was very ugly and dark. I was so frightened when I looked around, and saw how lonely and big it was. After that I can't remember anything for a long while. Then it seemed to me I woke again, very thin and white, and too weak even to cry, and my father came to me, and asked if I recollected him. But his face was quite strange to me, and I told him so; but he was so angry when I said this, that I never dared say it again. 'It is only the fever you have had makes you fancy me a stranger,' he said. 'Mind that, boy, and never let me hear such nonsense again.'"

"How very curious," said Lydia, "that in a fever you should forget your father's face."

Alfred gazed at her with bewildered eyes, very earnest and inquiring.

"Do you think so?" he asked. "My father told me, too, that I had never slept in a room with angels looking down upon me; it was only a dream in the fever, and I ought to forget it. But if that be true, there were many other dreams which came, too, I suppose in my illness, but which I can't forget."

"Were they pretty dreams?" asked Lydia, with intense curiosity.

"I can't tell you," replied Alfred, sorrowfully; "when I try to put them into words, they fly away. They come sometimes like pictures, when I am half sleeping, half waking; but if I rouse myself to think of them, they break in pieces, and I see only the great cold school-room, the desks and forms, and Mr. Whalley's cruel face. It was when my father left me at his school, that I cried worst of all; there too I left off crying. We had no garden, no quiet place to cry in; the boys, when they first came, used to lean their heads upon their desks and cry there, but they soon left off. We all got too desperate, I think, for crying. Sometimes the bigger boys would talk together of revenging themselves on Mr. Whalley; but the moment they caught a glimpse of his face, they were frightened and quiet. Oh, he is such a wicked, cruel man! I hate to remember him."

Lydia's tears remained suspended in her eyes as she listened to this history of woes and terrors, of which her happy childhood knew nothing.

"Never mind him now," she said. "He can't come here: you'll never see that wicked Mr. Whalley again."

But as if her words had conjured him from the deep, Alfred's eyes at that moment became fixed upon his face. Terror-stricken and mute, he seized Lydia's arm, and pointed between the roots and branches of the laurels out into the park. And there crawling slowly along the road, she saw a lean half-starved horse, a tall yellow gig, and a man with a hard face, and fierce eyes, who peered to the right and left, as with deliberate strokes he plied his whip on the lean steed's back.

Seated as they were on the bank, the children were just on a level with that portion of the laurel hedge—the twisted roots and trunks, through which alone it was possible to get a glimpse of the park; but Mr. Whalley, on the other hand, could see nothing of the garden, as his vision of course fell on the thickest part of the green wall.

"He is come for me," whispered Alfred, with pale lips. "Oh, Lydia, what shall I do?"

"Papa wont let him take you," returned the child, bravely; "and we'll set the dogs at him."

But, young as he was, the little Alfred had learned in a sharp school of misery to estimate character, and he knew instinctively that Lord Crehylls would give him up.

"Your mamma would not let that wicked man take me away; but your papa will," he said, as he clasped his hands tightly together. "Lydia, I wont go with him—I'll die first. Good-bye. I'll run away before he gets to the castle."

The little resolute face, so full of mingled terror and courage, bent towards her, and kissed her; and then Lydia, letting her flowers fall, seized him with both hands.

"He'll overtake you if you run away," she said, eagerly. "Better hide till he is gone. I know a hollow tree in the park : and if you creep in there, he'll never, never find you ; and in the evening, when he is gone, I'll come and tell you ; then you can stay with me again, and we'll be brother and sister always. Isn't that better than saying good-bye ? And, besides, he'll be sure to catch you if you run away."

" But if they ask you questions, Lydia, and frighten you, you will be obliged to tell where I am," said Alfred.

" Shall I ? No, never ! " returned the little creature, resolutely. " If you are sure I wont tell, will you wait in the tree till I come to you ? "

" Yes, I promise you that, Lydia," he answered.

" Then I'll be cut in pieces before I tell," she cried. " Come quickly, and I'll show you the tree."

She seized his hand, and together they ran out of the tall gates which shut in the quiet garden, and then went swiftly down a steep dell in the park beyond, where the trees soon hid them from sight.

Meanwhile, the yellow gig with the worn-out horse had crept on towards the castle, it still having three-quarters of a mile to go, when its hideous vision had fallen on the children's frightened eyes. Mr. Whalley, moreover, being of a cringing and vulgar nature, was overawed by the great park and the big castle ; hence he ceased to hurry the movements of the wretched animal that called him master. In fact, he was beginning to quail at the thought of finding himself face to face with the owner of Castle Crehylls. There were unpleasant memories connected with this name still seething in that caldron, his heart ; and unless some very strong motive had drawn him, he would not willingly have travelled this road. But he trusted to time, and above all to the respectability around him now, to defeat all prying eyes ; so, grimly smiling, he gathered up his courage, and driving to the door of Castle Crehylls, he laid his gaunt hand upon the bell. The servant who replied to the summons, scanned the yellow gig with some contempt, but stood silent while Mr. Whalley delivered himself of his name and his business.

"It is far from my wish to trouble his lordship at such a sad time," said Mr. Whalley; "therefore, if you will mention that I am come for the boy who ran away from my school about three weeks ago, and who I have ascertained is here, perhaps he will give you orders to deliver him up to me ; and in that case there will be no necessity for me to intrude further on his lordship."

Without any comment, and bearing Mr. Whalley's card with him, with the precise amount of disrespect it merited, the servant retired,

17—2

quickly returning to say that Lord Crehylls would see Mr. Whalley.

Ushered into the library, he found that helpless nobleman vainly striving to forget his anguish in the pages of Hobbes and Brown.

"Take a seat, Mr. Singleton," he said; "you are come for little Lanyon, I hear."

"Lanyon!" repeated Mr. Whalley, and his hard face took a strangely ashen hue; "I know no one of that name. I am come, my lord, for a boy called Alfred Singleton, a child of a strangely perverse disposition, whom his father—he has no mother—has intrusted to my care. My own name, my lord, is Whalley."

His voice quavered slightly as he spoke, and he glanced round the room in a hurried suspicious way.

"I beg your pardon," said Lord Crehylls; "I remember now the boy told me that his name was Singleton, but I imagined he was related to the Lanyons—that is, to the family of my brother's widow, the Dowager Lady Crehylls."

Mr. Whalley's face was ashen white now, and his nerveless hands fell down by his side.

"I know nothing of that lady, or of her family, my lord," he said. "The boy Single-ton has no relatives in England, and his father is quite of an inferior station. Perhaps your lordship will be good enough to order a servant to bring the child to me at once. Here is his guardian Mrs. Singleton's letter, desiring that he may be given into my charge."

Lord Crehylls took the letter in his helpless hands, and turned it over and over.

" I assure you," he said, " Lady Crehylls never anticipated your coming hither for the child, and I doubt if she would have yielded him into your hands."

A spasm passed over his face as he mentioned his wife's name, and for a moment his voice was choked, then he went on in a clearer voice.

" I have no doubt she knew all about the boy, or she would not have taken him in as she did. I never asked her anything; I left all things to her; but I certainly understood it was her intention to send him on to Penkivel in a few days, when he had rested, and therefore I naturally concluded he was in some way connected with the Lanyons. And—and, with your permission, I should prefer carrying out my poor wife's wishes; then, if Lady Crehylls of Penkivel chooses to give the child into your charge, I shall have nothing to say against it."

Lord Crehylls continued to twist the letter between his fingers as he spoke, while all the grief and agitation he repressed showed so plainly on his pale face, that any other man but Mr. Whalley would have pitied him.

" Considering that I have Mrs. Singleton's express commands to take her ward back to my school, at Exeter," observed the schoolmaster, " I do not see how I can possibly accede to your lordship's request, as it appears to me the journey to Penkivel would be useless expense and trouble. I can assure you, my lord, on my own certain knowledge, Lady Crehylls has not the shadow of a claim to interfere between Mrs. Singleton and her ward, the boy being in no way either related, or known to the Lanyons."

The utterance of this name seemed to scorch Mr. Whalley like the searing of a red-hot iron, for his face burst into a perspiration as he spoke it, and he wiped his brow with a shaking hand. Lord Crehylls, however, did not notice him ; his thoughts were with his dead wife — with her whose watchful love had, even to the last day of her life, taken all trouble from off his helpless hands.

" I cannot express to you," he said, " how obliged I shall feel, if you will nevertheless let the boy go to Penkivel. Lady Crehylls wished it, and I am sure you can understand how much any wish of hers——" He broke down here, then recovered himself, laying his hand feebly upon his book, and going on in a lower voice—" any wish of hers must weigh with me now. And although you assure me, there is no relationship between the little Singleton and the Lanyon family, I am inclined to think there must be some strong friendship or other tie between his family and hers, otherwise———"

"Your lordship is mistaken," interrupted Mr. Whalley. "Mrs. Singleton would have told me so had such been the case."

"But there can be no objection to the child's going to Penkivel," persisted Lord Crehylls. "The journey shall be no expense or trouble to you. I will give orders to have a carriage got ready, and my servant shall drive you and the boy down there together."

"My lord, you are very good," said Mr. Whalley, wiping the perspiration again from his face, "and I am grieved I cannot accept your proposition; but Mrs. Singleton's letter expressly forbids it. If you will take the trouble to read her words, you will see they are very peremptory."

Again, Lord Crehylls twisted the letter in his fingers, and at length exerted himself to read the few sharp lines, in which Mrs. Singleton desired that her run-away brother and ward, if he had taken refuge at Crehylls, should be delivered up to his schoolmaster, Mr. Whalley."

The decisive tone of the letter conquered the dreamy bookworm to whom it was addressed. Poor Lord Crehylls! Had he lived to these days of examinations, he would certainly have passed for anything and everything; but he had not a single quality by which the battle of life can be fought or won.

"I certainly wished," he said, weakly yielding the point, "to send the child to Penkivel; but since his guardians desire otherwise, I do not see that I can interfere further."

"Certainly not, my lord," said Mr. Whalley. "Will you permit me to ring, and desire that the boy may be brought to me?"

But when this was done, and the servant had received his orders, there followed a long pause, during which Lord Crehylls dived into the thickest mataphysics, emerging with a great effort to be courteous to the schoolmaster, then plunging again, and thus, for a few happy minutes, dulling his mind to the pain of knowing himself lonely, bereaved, and helpless.

"The little gentleman is not to be found anywhere, my lord," said the servant, appearing at the door with a frightened countenance.

At this news, Mr. Whalley started up with a face livid with suppressed rage. In any other place, in any other presence, he would have shown himself the fiend he was; but here he felt obliged to restrain himself.

Lord Crehylls closed his book in great annoyance.

"Not to be found!" he exclaimed. "Do you know, Grylls, for whom I am asking?"

"For the young gentleman, whom my lady brought home with her, my lord, about a week ago," returned Grylls. "We have searched the house and the gardens, my lord, but we can't find him. Mrs. Richards thinks he has run away again."

Mrs. Richards was the nurse.

"Send Mrs. Richards and my daughter to me," said Lord Crehylls.

"The servants are all in a conspiracy!" burst forth Mr. Whalley. "They have hidden the boy themselves, but they had better take care what they are about. I am not a man to be trifled with."

During this speech, Grylls, who was an old man, grey and bent, fixed his eyes earnestly on Mr. Whalley's hard features, an expression of bewilderment and fear gradually over-spreading his face. Then, without a word, he backed to the door, went out, and closed it softly.

"If ghosts walked and talked, I should say he was a ghost," muttered Grylls, as he crossed the hall; "but there! that's nonsense. Buried men don't rise again."

*   *   *   *   *   *

Mrs. Richards had been questioned and dismissed. She had conducted the children to the garden, and left them there; the little boy she had not seen since. Miss Lydia had returned to the house alone. This was the substance of her evidence.

" Then, my pretty little miss," said Mr. Whalley, in his most fawning tone, " you know all about it, don't you? You'll tell me where the boy is gone."

" I shall tell nothing," returned Lydia, resolutely. " You are a cruel, wicked man. Alfred has told me so. And I should be wicked too if I helped you to find him."

Mr. Whalley tried to smile at this language; but he failed in the effort, and ground his teeth together to keep down his rising rage.

" Alfred Singleton is a lying, bad boy," he said ; " and I see he has made you as naughty as himself."

" Sir," observed Lord Crehylls, " I prefer to rebuke my daughter myself when she merits it ; and I will question her myself also, if you please."

Cringing instantly, like a beaten hound, Mr. Whalley sat uneasily on the edge of his chair, gnawing his fingers in silence. Then Lord Crehylls, in a futile, perplexed way, proceeded to question his little daughter ; but Lydia was true to her trust. The child who has never heard a word of unkindness, or felt a blow, is fearless as a lion, and rarely, very rarely indeed, untruthful. Thus, without any evasion, she continued to answer, in the softest of little flute-like voices, that she had promised not to tell ; and therefore wondered, with small dignified surprise, how her father could suppose it possible that she would break her word.

Lord Crehylls was puzzled. The chivalry, the honour, the truth, and courage that live, or should live in gentle blood, shone in the brave eyes of his little daughter, as she looked him trustfully in the face; and he could not force her to belie her nature. Secretly he was proud of her steadfastness, and glad that neither threats nor promises had shaken it.

"I do not see that I can do anything further, sir," he said, turning to Mr. Whalley. "Since my little girl has made a promise, I cannot oblige her to break it."

If Mr. Whalley could have fulfilled his own desires at that moment, he would have roasted the child at a slow fire till she divulged the truth; but not being able to glut his cruelty or his rage, he could only say, with his face at a white heat, that he considered Miss Crehylls was bound to tell where Alfred Singleton was.

"He is my friend," cried little Lydia, with her cheeks all aflame. "Mamma told me to be his friend; and she told me, too, always to keep a promise. I wont disobey mamma, now she is gone to heaven. I love mamma, and will always try to obey her while I live; but I hate wicked men, who kill poor little children, as ogres do, and I shall never do anything that they tell me."

Her eyes flashing with a generous fire, she confronted Mr. Whalley with a bravery which he longed to wrench out of her heart with a cruel hand. But she was Lord Crehylls' daughter; she was as far out of his reach as the stars, so he could only cringe again, steadying his nether lip with teeth set firmly on it.

"I perceive, my lord," said he, "that this runaway pupil of mine has added falsehood and slander to his other misdeeds. I shall spare him no more. I confess now that he is a thief. He has stolen money and jewels from my house —this was the cause of his flight—and doubtless he has his plunder with him."

He glanced at Lydia as he spoke. The child remained steadfast, but she turned very pale. To her innocence, guarded as it was by an atmosphere of purity, honour, and gentleness, the idea of theft was appalling. Dwelling among a simple people, with whom the sin was and is rare, the thought brought a horror with it scarcely comprehensible perhaps to a city child, to whose mind the crime would not be so dim, so shadowy, so unfamiliar.

"You are making a grave accusation, sir," observed Lord Crehylls. "Are you prepared to sustain it?"

"I grieve to say I am, my lord," replied Mr. Whalley; "and I grieve further that, in the cause of justice, I feel compelled to seek the nearest magistrate, and to demand a warrant for the apprehension of Alfred Singleton. I fear, my lord, the officers will search Castle Crehylls."

He glanced furtively at the meek dreamer whom he thus threatened, but he, lost in his own grief, scarcely understood him.

"Search Castle Crehylls!" he repeated. "Ah yes, but the servants say they have looked for the boy everywhere. At any other time, sir, you should be welcome to search with them, but really now—when—when Lady Crehylls——"

He could not finish the sentence, but looked out dreamily upon the sunny lawn, with a mist of tears rising to his eyes.

"Then I take my leave, my lord, understanding that you prohibit any further search," said Mr. Whalley, rising; "and I must of course take my own means to recover the little villain, who has robbed me."

Steadfastly regarding him still, Lydia laid her hand upon her father's arm, and pointed with the other to Mr. Whalley's face.

"He looks like the picture of Crook-backed Richard, who killed the little children in the Tower," she whispered. "Do not believe a word he says, papa; Alfred is no thief. The man is a thief and a murderer himself: he beat one poor boy to death not long ago."

Each word of her childish whisper fell upon Mr. Whalley's ear, withering every semblance of manhood from out his face; thus it happened, that when Lord Crehylls turned his eyes on him, he saw, as in a mist, a dreadful mask, portraying abject fear and hatred; and behind this mask there gleamed upon the dreamy nobleman a face, which vanished ere the sight had time to fix it in the memory. Yet, when Mr. Whalley had bowed himself to the door, and had departed from the castle with an unspoken curse upon his lips, some shadowy remembrance of that face flitted still before the dreamy eyes of the sorrow-stricken Lord Crehylls.

CHAPTER XXII

T was not until the morning that Madeline glanced at the note, which the Duke de Briancourt had placed within the flowers. When she read it, she grew first thoughtful, then contemptuous; but her scorn did not hinder her hand from trembling, as she held it out to greet him on his arrival. The duke spoke English, French, and Italian, equally well. A Russian has the gift of tongues, and masters a foreign language with wonderful facility. He addressed Madeline in English, and for a short time conversed only on common topics. Then suddenly he changed his language to Italian, and with it his manner also.

"Madeline," he said, "I have loved you too long to play a farce like this. I cannot converse on indifferent subjects. Tell me, do you intend still to refuse my request?"

Madeline's face grew white to the lips as he asked this question, and there flashed into her eyes an indescribable look of fear and sorrow; yet she answered him in a quiet tone of perfect civility and self-possession.

"I certainly do not feel myself at liberty to accede to it, duke."

"May I ask your reasons?" he demanded, as a dusky flush swept over his thin cheeks.

"Why should I tell you my reasons?" she returned. "Why should I close my doors to the only friend I have? Am I not at liberty to receive what guests I please?"

"No," said he, savagely; "I allow you no such liberty, except at the cost of destruction to all your long fostered schemes of vengeance against the woman you hate."

"Do you threaten me?" asked Madame Silvia, in her softest voice. "This is a new way of making love."

"Neither my love nor my threats are new to you," returned the duke, grasping his chair nervously. "Madeline Sylvester, you shall keep your promises to me, or I will let Maurice Pellew know wherefore, and in what I was your accomplice. You see I read easily the dearest secret of your heart."

As he said this, with his fierce eyes fixed on her moodily, the blood rushed in a crimson flood to her face, neck, and bosom, leaving her, as it hurried back to her heart, white as marble.

"I have touched you there," said the duke, smiling triumphantly; but in his triumph there was mingled so much pain, so much bitterness, for himself, that, unable to bear the sight of her emotion, he turned away and set his teeth firmly together.

Madeline seemed more fearful of the duke's jealousy than of his love. Perhaps she feared the latter only for herself, and the first for Maurice.

"You are right," she said, mournfully. "Your words have touched me; but not for the cause you think. Am I a woman who could dare to love a good man? Maurice Pellew can never be anything to me. Your threat agitated me, because, if you fulfilled it, you would destroy all I live for—justice."

"Is not your thirsty heart satiated yet?" returned the duke. "Lord Crehylls is dead, and his wife a widow, and childless. Is not that enough?"

His voice had a strange ring in it; and their eyes met—his smiling; hers dry and fierce.

"Enough!" she said. "You use the word, who do not know my wrongs. Nothing I can make her suffer will ever equal the anguish she has heaped on me."

With her hand upon her heart, as though some sudden pang had seized it, she started up and paced the room hurriedly. The duke watched her with eyes that seemed to devour the grace of her movements, and the wonderful beauty of her face.

"Madeline," he said, softly, "forgive me. It is only when I am jealous that I lose my senses, and threaten you. Believe me, I will not betray you. Only promise me that you will never give Maurice Pellew your love."

"Why should I bestow on him a gift that would be a curse?" she cried, turning on him fiercely. "I would tear the beauty out of my face with my own hands, rather than let my miserable heart love Maurice Pellew."

The duke did not perceive that the woman who could say this had already given her love; he saw only that his rival had no better chance than himself, and his jealousy was appeased.

"Enough!" he said, eagerly. "I want no more assurances. I know you were still almost a child when you were going to take this man, this Pellew, for your husband; and I have no doubt, if ever you had any love for him, it long since died out of your heart."

"I killed it," returned Madeline, looking him in the face, "when I married Thomas Singleton. Yes, you are right—it is dead; it can never rise again to torment me and show me what I have done, and what I have lost, for the sake of justice."

"Then, Madeline," cried the duke, eagerly, "why not accept my love, my tenderness, my life-long devotion?"

" Are you asking me to be your wife ?" said Madeline, in a calm, cold tone.

" No, but I am praying you to let me be your slave," replied the duke. " You know, that in a little Russian village there lives a simple, ignorant woman, who calls me her husband. While she lives I cannot offer you marriage, Madeline."

" But you can refrain from insulting me," she responded, in the same calm way. " Not that I heed you, for your words make no more impression on my mind than a snowflake does upon the sea."

" Say the icy sea, and the simile will be more perfect," added the duke ; " but do not rave of insults. Had not Lord Crehylls a wife ? And many people say you left England for his sake."

As Madeline heard him, her face turned white as the snow of which she had spoken, and rising, she came and stood before him like a cold statue.

" When I hear such words as these, I know what my mercy towards that man has cost me," she said. " It permits such a man as you to insult me—a man who has won rank and seeming honour by the deepest treachery,—a man who, whether paid by France or Russia, was ever a spy and a traitor."

Beside himself with rage, the duke seized her by the wrists, but she did not struggle in his

18—2

grasp; perfectly unmoved and calm, she went on, bearing unflinchingly a clasp in which her very soul writhed.

"During the war you were a paid spy; poorly paid at first; but found so useful, that your master thought it wise to give you rank and wealth, that, by these passports, you might enter palaces, and betray their inmates, just as you had hitherto betrayed less noble friends. Alexis Sobraski, Duke de Briancourt, I am not afraid of you; and I intend you to understand, once and for ever, that I would not endure an insult from a royal duke, a duke of a hundred descents, much less from such a duke as you!"

The contempt with which she spoke might have scorched him, could he have been destroyed by scorn; but the man who can endure to take the office of a spy is not likely to be withered by a woman's contempt.

"Whatever I may be," he said, coldly, "I was not too mean to be your friend. Take care you do not make me your enemy."

He dropped her wrists, which he had reddened with his grasp, and leant back on his seat with an air of calm power. His touch had irritated Madeline almost to madness; a moment ago she had stood before him trembling with rage, but now she quailed, and tears started to her eyes.

"I have no wish to make you my enemy," she

said; "but I demand from you the conduct of a gentleman, not of a ruffian. Why insult me with words you know I will not endure?"

"Why persist in calling my long, patient love an insult?" returned the duke. "I have told you all my history. I have confessed to you that I was born a serf, and married, when a boy, to a woman I hated. The chain is odious to me; it makes me hateful in your sight; it brings my love before you as a thing to be contemned, to be repulsed with horror. It gives you the right to despise me, while it always leaves me the maddening hope that these shackles alone are the cause of your contempt; and if I were free, I might win you. Madeline! Madeline! have some pity on a heart which has given you such a long-suffering, enduring love."

As he spoke, Madeline put out her hands before her eyes, blindly; her frame trembled—her lips shook.

"I could be sorry for a hopeless love," she said, softly; "but I have known a love more long-suffering than yours,—a love as gentle, as patient, as worthy, as yours is impatient and unworthy; and I cannot forget, that, when I was maddened by the loss of that love, you and your wretched friend Rathline came to me and tempted me. Then it was I chose vengeance, and took ruin with it."

Sinking into a chair, she covered her face with

her hands, while the heaving of her bosom betrayed a grief stronger than her words. The duke gazed at her at first doubtfully, then with a strange gleam flashing into his light eyes.

"Are you struck with remorse?" he said— "you, who take revenge, and call it justice! Are you going to turn back in weakness?"

"Say no more to me now," returned Madeline, as her hands dropped from her face, and showed it ghastly white; "I cannot bear another word."

"Let me say one only," urged the duke. "Madeline, shackled as I am, you will not give me the torture of accepting another?"

"How can you fear such a thing?" she answered, mournfully. "Have I not sacrificed all happiness and all love? Is Madeline Sherborne a woman who can hope for a good man's respect?"

"Your beauty and genius have made men half mad," he rejoined, in a gloomy tone. "Who has cared whether you were good or bad, when they have looked upon your face?"

This man's compliments were like himself, saturnine; and his insane and moody passion was dangerous, and Madeline knew it; so she strove to soothe him, and with some success, for when he quitted her, his restless eyes and his haggard face wore somewhat of a brighter look. As she listened to his retreating steps she glanced at the time-piece breathlessly. In a few minutes Maurice Pellew would be here. What if they should meet? The thought made her tremble, and she went hastily to the window and looked out into the hot street, where long trails of sunshine, dust-laden, struggled with the heavy shadows that fell from roof and chimney. At the door the duke's horses stood fretting, and as he gathered up the reins he glanced upwards, and the light fell upon his keen, thin, and powerful face. Madeline shuddered, yet she forced her lips into a smile; then the showy carriage and the great black horses pranced away.

"And that man, too, I suffer, for the sake of this hard justice!" said Madeline to herself, bitterly. "Father, can your agony only be avenged at the cost of honour, happiness, and life?"

She sank down upon her knees, and gave way to a burst of sorrow; yet it lasted but for a moment, and when she rose, she dashed away her tears, exclaiming scornfully, "Am I a fool, that I hesitate thus in weakness! No, I counted the cost of all this long ago. I have paid the penalty, and I will not go back."

As she spoke, she looked down upon the red marks still lingering on her wrists, and bit her lip in passionate anger.

"How dared he?" she cried to herself; "how

dared he touch me? When I put my hand into
Maurice Pellew's, I shall remember this degrading
touch. I shall shrink and shiver at it. I shall
feel that, if he knew it, he would think some of
my dishonour rested upon him, merely because
he entered my roof; and I should read again in
his eyes that pity which I hate."

At this instant a voice, a step, brought a rush
of colour to her face, and she fled precipitately.
Thus, when Maurice Pellew entered the room, he
found it empty.

Before she came back and greeted her guest,
Madeline changed her dress and jewels. She
flung off the rich toilette that had dazzled the
duke, and arrayed herself simply, almost girlishly;
but she strove vainly to fling off also her recol-
lection of the duke's insolent words, his terrible
love, and his cruel grasp; these memories were
with her when she clasped the hand of Maurice.
To her the room still seemed haunted by the
presence of the man whose relentless passion
had pursued her for so many years; and, turning
from the window, she avoided the chair on which
he had sat, the table on which he had leaned,
and the book he had opened.

" Madeline," said Maurice, coming forward to
meet her, " you are pale to-night. You are not
strong enough for the excitement and fatigue of
the stage."

" What does that matter?" she answered, carelessly. "While I can bear it, I shall go on; and when voice and health fail, I shall wring a living, in some other way, from this hard world."

"But surely you have a competence?" said Maurice, in an embarrassed tone. "I thought your marriage with Mr. Singleton gave you your aunt's fortune?"

Madeline blushed, and then turned pale, as she always did at any mention of her husband's name.

"Yes, my marriage gave me that," she said; "but I give up the whole of the income derived from that poor twelve thousand pounds to—to Tom's relations."

Although Tom Singleton was dead, Maurice Pellew's jealous heart could ill endure to hear Madeline name him with familiar kindness. His own prior right to her love made it seem strange, unnatural, that her lips should speak of this other man, this interloper, in tones of affection. To him it appeared as though they had been separated but a week, and her marriage and her widowhood were as a dream.

"What are Mr. Singleton's relations to you," he said, glancing at her half reproachfully, "that you should divest yourself of fortune, and follow an arduous profession to maintain them?"

"But for Tom's sake they are very little to me," she answered, "except Alice, whom I like for herself."

" And she can't want a large income ?" observed Maurice.

" No, but Mr. Rathline does," replied Madeline, with a nervous laugh.

" Is it possible that you permit yourself to be robbed by that villain ?" cried Maurice.

" Yes," she answered, throwing herself wearily into a chair; " all my triumphs represent so many guineas for Mr. Rathline. I sing for him, I act for him. For him I undertake the most arduous parts; for him I work early and late ; for him I rack heart and brain. But there are times when I weary of it all, Maurice."

Mr. Pellew heard her with an astonishment he could not utter.

" I had no idea," he said, " that you ever spoke to that scoundrel. I wonder he dares live upon you in this way."

" There are men," returned Madeline, " who have the art of making women work for them, and he is one. While there is a woman left in the world, Richard Rathline will never earn a meal by the sweat of his own brow."

" But what claim has this swaggerer on you ?" cried Maurice, impatiently. " If he wrings money from the weakness of a wife or a sister, you surely have the strength and the right to resist him."

Something in this speech made Madeline turn pale.

"Nevertheless, Richard Rathline drains my purse," she said, evasively. "You forget he is the father of my ward. It is through that boy he claims a right to rob me," she added, with a bitter laugh.

"I was cruel to forget your anxiety," observed Maurice. "Is the poor child found?"

"He has been found, but is lost again," replied Madeline, with a blush of fire crimsoning her face; "that is, he was traced to Castle Crehylls——"

"To Castle Crehylls!" exclaimed Maurice. "How strange!"

"Not so very strange," returned Madeline, averting her face from his gaze. "Mr. Rathline took the boy to that neighbourhood some time ago, and I believe they saw my old enemy, Lady Crehylls, and — and perhaps the child liked her."

"It will be fortunate if the boy has taken refuge with Lady Crehylls," said Maurice. "Your anxiety will be set at rest then."

"On the contrary, it would be increased," replied Madeline, with marked coldness. "My dislike to my traducer has not diminished, although you of course are still her friend. I would rather the boy died than find a home with her."

Her words pained Maurice, as every reference to Lady Crehylls always did.

"Madeline, I wish you would learn to spare me," he said, with some weariness. "There are times when I try to forget the bitter past—times when I even do forget it for a brief moment,—but you ever, by some cruel word, bring back the old agony as freshly as if it had only crushed me yesterday."

Madeline listened, with her right hand clenched and her left raised to her brow, to shade her face from his view.

"I should be sorry," she said, putting her lips together with an effort, "if I ever forget the past for an instant. My memories are fresh. I remember keenly that my past and present have been shaped by the hand of Agatha Crehylls; I remember that I owe my marriage and my widowhood to her. She gave me Richard Rathline for a father-in-law, and she slandered me to Maurice Pellew, who believed her, and left me."

Maurice bore these words patiently.

"Who suffered most, Madeline," he said, "you or I? You married, and forgot me. I am single still."

"I married, and remembered," said Madeline, with quivering lips. "There was my sin. The question is not who suffered most, but who sinned most. Do you think there is no agony of remorse in my mind for the wrong I did to a noble heart?"

" If all your repentance is for Mr. Singleton," returned Maurice, coldly, " I will say no more. For my own part, I thought he had known how to take advantage of your anger to hurry you into a hasty marriage. If he was unhappy, I don't pity him."

" You do him an injustice," said Madeline, looking up with sudden tears shining in her eyes. " I proposed our marriage to him myself."

" Did you?" asked Maurice, with a great hot flush springing to his face. " I should scarcely have credited you with such an act."

" I did it," she answered, " impulsively, as I do all things. I did it from impatience, weariness, anger, fear, gratitude—every feeling there is in the heart, except love. And yet, if I had had a brother—an only brother born the same hour with myself—he would not have been dearer to me than Tom Singleton was."

" What a theme to talk of to me!" thought Maurice to himself. " But don't widows always weary us with praises of the departed? I was foolish enough to believe," he said, looking at her earnestly, " that your love for me was even greater than this. I was not prepared for the unforgiving, relentless spirit, in which you wrecked my happiness."

" I was insulted, calumniated, forsaken," she said ; " and, in my pride and bitterness, I resolved to make it a duty to crush my love for you out of my heart. So I married ; and you, of all men, have no right to reproach me."

Her sudden wildness startled Mr. Pellew.

" We will not speak any more of this," he said, turning the pages of a book hurriedly. " It is only the old story, which I have explained so often. I was to blame, but I could not dream that your resentment would lead you into an act so hasty and irremediable."

" Don't you know me yet ?" she asked, half wistfully. " My nature is too impatient for wearying and waiting. I act impulsively, and repent afterwards."

She finished with a laugh, and then crossed her arms on her bosom, as if to hold down a rising sob. For a moment a dead silence crept over them, through which there passed many a shadow of earlier, happier years.

" I am a coward," said Maurice, breaking the silence in a trembling voice. " I have no right to remind you of your sorrows or your faults. Of my own choice I came here as your friend ; and having accepted that position, I know I ought not to rake up the ashes of a dead past, to make them a subject of reproach ; and even if I had a hope of being something dearer than a friend, I should find in that no right to utter a word to pain you. Madeline, is there such a hope for me?"

Madeline gazed at him with great wistful eyes, into which there grew the shadow of unshed tears; then she turned away, hiding her face.

"There is no hope," she said, calmly. "There is an unseen barrier between us, Maurice, and I cannot overstep it."

"If you allude to the affair of Lord Crehylls," he said, eagerly, "I have already told you, Madeline, that I guess it all."

She turned and looked at him with flushed cheeks, and eyes full of terror.

"All!" she cried, hurriedly. "What do you mean?"

"Lord Crehylls wrote to me when he first went abroad, putting before me a supposed case, which I guessed to be his own," replied Maurice.

"When he first went abroad!" repeated Madeline; "and he did not write after—after the death of his child?"

"No, I have not heard from him for years. But why should Lord Crehylls, innocent or guilty, separate you and me?" he asked, earnestly.

"It was his wife who separated us," replied Madeline; "it is she who still separates us. She had no right to part us when she did, but perhaps she would have the right now. But I will never give her the power."

"Do you think I am so mad that I should ever listen again to Lady Crehylls?" said Maurice, passionately.

"Yes, you would listen," returned Madeline, sorrowfully; "and you would forsake me again —perhaps this time justly. You blamed me once, when I thought I did not merit blame; I do not hold myself guiltless now."

"I considered you presumptuous," said Maurice, eagerly, "in forcing Lord Crehylls to quit England on a charge which was not proved; but your youth, the circumstances of your father's death, and the confession which Lord Crehylls doubtless made of the rash blow he struck Carbis, are great excuses for you. Knowing the whole case, as I do now, I can safely assure you, Madeline, that it can never again be made a cause of quarrel between you and me."

"You are mistaken," she returned. "There are circumstances arising from it, unknown to you, which stand like a wall between us. These would make a deadly breach between you and me, whether whispered to you by friend or foe?"

Her tone was so cold, her manner so constrained, that Maurice felt a chill pass over him, and the passionate words rising to his lips died there unspoken. It seemed impossible to speak tenderly to a woman of ice and marble.

"If you are resolved to think so," he said, "all assurances of mine to the contrary would be useless."

There was a strange look in Madeline's eyes as her sad gaze met his.

"Useless, indeed," she said. "Richard Rathline might tell me so, and I would believe him, but not you."

"Do you hold my word cheaper than a scoundrel's?" asked Maurice, in anger. "If so, it is vain indeed to speak."

"It is vain to speak of love," said Madeline. "I will never wrong a good man again. Let us be friends, Maurice, and forget all this for ever."

She held out her hand to him; he took it for a moment, then let it drop coldly. If she felt this, there was no change, no pique in her voice and manner when she addressed him again.

"Give me your advice, Maurice, about the boy," she said. "What measures shall I take to recover him?"

Then she told him of the schoolmaster's visit to Crehylls, and Alfred's second escape.

"Can he be gone to his father?" said Maurice.

"I am certain he is not," she replied.

"Where is Mr. Rathline?" he asked, carelessly. "I want to find him."

" I never know where he is, except when he needs money," she replied. " I can tell you when he next pulls hard at my purse, and you can see him then, if you will. But what is your business with Rathline ?"

" Suppose I have still a theory of my own respecting the death of Mathew Carbis," said Maurice, smiling ; " what then ?"

" Why, then, if it involves a supposition that Lord Crehylls' was not the hand that killed him, you are grievously wrong," returned Madeline, with a hot flush upon her face. " If Lord Crehylls is innocent, I am the most miserable and guilty woman in the world. Bu why do I speak of this ? Such a thought is folly."

" It is no folly," said Maurice ; " it is too likely to be a truth. Madeline, last night you remarked that you repented of your romance. Why not prove your repentance by aiding me to unravel this mystery ?"

Madeline was silent. Her convictions were too strong, too firmly rooted, to be shaken by any argument Maurice might use ; nevertheless, his doubts irritated her, and going to her desk, she unlocked it, and laid her father's letter before him.

" Since Lord Crehylls himself told you his history," she said, " I do not think I am breaking my promise of silence in showing you this. You know I kept my word, even through loss of love and happiness."

Maurice could not read the letter penned by
Walter Sherborne without emotion, nor without
finding his own theory greatly shaken by his
perusal of it. Madeline's conduct, too, struck
him in another light, and he no longer wondered
at her sentence on Lord Crehylls; he only re-
gretted it.

"A trial would have brought out the truth,"
he said to himself. "And yet, if this letter is
untrue, its cruelty is past belief. Madeline," he
said, taking her hand, "your love for Mr. Lanyon
must have been very great, since for his sake you
forbore to ruin his daughter, and his son-in-
law?"

"And you know how Lady Crehylls rewarded
me!" she said, bitterly. "I showed mercy to
her husband, but I mean to deal out justice to
her."

"Does she know this story?" asked Maurice.

"Partly," replied Madeline. "I sent Richard
Rathline to her about two years ago—the time
he had the child with him—and he told her some
of the mournful truth. He made her understand
that I only exiled her husband, when I might
have exposed his guilt to a gaping world, and he
informed her also that I had promised to be
silent, and had kept my word even when she
slandered me."

"She has had a sad life," said Maurice.

"She has kept her name and her honour," returned Madeline, in a hard voice : " she left me neither. If her life has been unhappy, mine has been bitter. You waste your pity strangely on this woman, Maurice."

"Do I ?" he said, quietly. " And yet I never forget, Madeline, that she parted us by her foolish jealousy,—a harder thing for me to forgive than you."

Madeline was silent, but Maurice did not mention Agatha Crehylls again.

" You must promise to let me see Rathline when he comes here again," he said. "Madeline, he added, suddenly, " did you ever hear him name a friend of his, called Whalley ?"

" Whalley !" repeated Madeline, in surprise.

But here Alice Rathline's voice broke suddenly upon their interview, and Alice's face was presented abruptly at the door.

" I begin to think you don't mean to have any dinner," she said. " I have been sounding the gong with all my might these five minutes."

END OF VOL. II.

www.ingramcontent.com/pod-product-compliance
Lightning Source LLC
Chambersburg PA
CBHW020848020726
47497CB00005B/1303